BOUND TO GODS

THEIR DARK VALKYRIE #2

EVA CHASE

INK SPARK PRESS

Bound to Gods

Book 2 in the Their Dark Valkyrie series

First Digital Edition, 2018

Copyright © 2018 Eva Chase

Cover design: Rebecca Frank

Ebook ISBN: 978-1-989096-15-4

Paperback ISBN: 978-1-989096-16-1

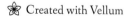 Created with Vellum

1

Aria

You'd think the realm of the gods would be a glorious place, right? All warmth and sunlight and beauty. But as I wandered across the vast vacant courtyard at the edge of Asgard, the gold-gilded stone walls of Valhalla looming at my right and the marble tiles ringing out with my and my companions' footsteps, I wasn't sure I'd ever been anywhere that felt quite this desolate or haunted before. A cool breeze tickled over my bare arms, raising goosebumps.

Of course, maybe the *actual* Asgard would have met my expectations. This was a fake one that I'd been brought to by a fake Odin, along with the four gods who'd summoned me to be their Valkyrie, and Odin's wife, the goddess Freya. All of whom looked just as unsettled by the fake-Odin's recent crumbling-into-dust routine as I was.

"The details all look right," Freya said. She swept her honey-brown waves back behind her shoulders as she took in the space. Her normally smooth forehead was creased with worry. "How could anyone have recreated Asgard this well?"

"*Have* they even recreated all of it?" asked Loki. The trickster's amber eyes flashed. "If you'll all excuse me for a moment..."

He sprang off the ground, his magical shoes allowing him to walk as if flying. In an instant, his tall lanky form had sped away from us into the distance where a whole city of smaller—but still pretty epic—stone halls stood. His pale red hair whipped like a flame in the wind he'd stirred up. He paused so far down one of the marble walkways that I could barely make out his green tunic against the trees beyond him. Then he spun and whisked back to us, his angular face set with a frown.

"Well?" Thor said in a growl of a baritone. He was still testing the weight of Mjolnir, his godly hammer, in his hand as if looking for something—or someone—to smash with it. The muscles in his beefy arms flexed. "What did you find?"

"It appears to be a rather thorough replica," Loki said. "All the halls, the orchard and the Norns' forest beyond... Someone has gone to a lot of trouble at our expense. I'd almost be flattered if it wasn't a very thorough *prison*."

My arms itched to hug myself, but I kept them stiff at my sides. "Is there any way out with the bridge gone?" The rainbow bridge fake-Odin had called up, to lead us who-knew-where that wasn't actually Asgard. My throat tightened.

I'd only left the world I'd grown up in, the human realm the gods called Midgard, because there wasn't much of a place for me there anymore. Technically, I'd already died there. The gods had called me back into being as a valkyrie after I'd been crushed by a speeding druggie-driven jeep. But I'd been starting to find a sort of home among the gods as they'd taught me to use the valkyrie powers they'd given me... and as they'd started to mean more to me than almost anyone back home, all of them, in their own ways.

Almost anyone. I'd left behind my little brother, who I'd nearly died all over again protecting. Petey didn't remember me anymore, a fact that sat in my gut like a hard peach pit I'd accidentally swallowed. Hod, god of cold and darkness, had wiped his mind and wiped the memories of him from everyone who'd known him except for me. After our enemies had threatened him to get to me, it'd been the only solution we could see to keep him safe.

I'd come to Asgard with the promise I'd still get to watch over Petey from afar. If he'd been in danger again I could have intervened. Not while I was shut up in some shiny prison, though.

"If it were the real Asgard, there'd be other doorways," Loki said. "But somehow I doubt that whoever arranged for us to end up here plans on letting us waltz right back out."

"Not after they've gone to this much trouble," Freya murmured in agreement.

Thor set his strong hand on my shoulder. "There'll be

a way out, Ari. If we can't find one waiting for us, we'll just have to bash our way out."

The trickster raised an eyebrow at him. "I'm sure you'd enjoy that too, Thunderer."

"Where's the raven woman?" Hod asked. "I haven't heard her among us since before that false Allfather fell." He trained his dark green eyes toward the others with his usual intensity, but he couldn't see them any more than he could have seen Muninn, Odin's raven of memory, who'd helped us with the rescue. Supposedly helped us, anyway.

"I haven't seen her since just after we arrived," Baldur said, his voice as dreamily bright as his shaggy white-blond hair. Despite being twins, he and Hod were a study in opposites. Both were strikingly good-looking, like all the gods seemed to be, with a boyishness to their faces and a height that didn't quite reach Loki's or Thor's, but that was as far as the resemblance went. Baldur was brawny and soft and glowing with the light he ruled over. Hod was lean and hard and shadowy.

Their personalities had plenty of contrast too. Baldur smiled gently as he took in the courtyard. "Perhaps she's searching for answers as we are."

Hod made a skeptical sound. "Maybe she *has* the answers, and she has no intention of sharing them. She's the one who led us to Odin in the dark elves' caves, isn't she? She was *his* raven. How could she not have known something was wrong?"

His blind glower was as dark as his short black hair, but I knew there was more to him than grim snarkiness. Hod kept his tender side tightly under wraps. I'd gotten close enough to see it—and to get a taste of just how tender he could be.

"None of us knew," Loki pointed out. "I'm his sworn blood-brother. The three of you are his sons. Freya's his wife. All of us should have realized. But only Ari did." He cocked his head at me. "Interesting. What was it that tipped you off, pixie?"

The memory sent a shiver through me. "When you sent me to find Odin before, through Valhalla and Yggdrasil, I felt a pull to him." That was why they'd been conjuring valkyries—the three before me who'd failed as well as me. Apparently Odin had dismissed all the woman warriors he'd brought into his service a long time ago, but the gods had used their own ties to him to pass that bond on to me as if he'd resurrected me himself. "I didn't feel any sense of connection with this one. Not even in the caves. I just didn't realize what was missing right away."

"Hmm." The trickster spun on his heel. "I don't like this at all. Well, let's take a closer look around and see if we can't discover the raven's hiding place. We can give our valkyrie a little tour along the way."

"A tour of an Asgard that isn't really Asgard?" I said as the rest of us fell into step around Loki.

"It does look an awful lot like the real thing," Thor said beside me. He pointed toward one of the nearest halls, with a roof thatched with silver reeds. "I'd almost think that was my hall, my home... if I hadn't just watched my father crumple into a pile of dirt." The growl came back into his voice on the last few words.

Right. This trap must be just as painful for the gods

as it was for me—maybe even more. They'd been waiting decades to get back home, wondering why Odin hadn't returned from his travels on Midgard, unable to find him themselves. For just a moment they'd have thought they were finally back, and now they didn't even know where they were.

I did hug myself then. Nothing about this sat right. I had wings ready to sprout from my back, my switchblade in my pocket, and god-given strength, speed, and sharpened senses at my disposal—and I could do nothing with any of those things to make this situation better.

"Muninn!" Freya called out in her sweetly measured voice. "Come back to us. We should talk this over."

From the way her elegant hand rested on the hilt of the sword at her side, I wouldn't have blamed the raven woman for not believing that the goddess of love and war only wanted to talk.

"That great wall you can thank me for," Loki said, only a little tension in his jaunty tone as he pointed to the high stone wall that lay beyond the halls. "At least, if it were the real one, you could have. A little wagering, a little magic, and we got the whole thing for free."

Thor raised an eyebrow. "I seem to remember it being a little more complicated than that."

"You all almost paid our giant builder with my hand in marriage," Freya said archly. "An offer that got made a lot more often than I can say I appreciated."

"Ah, but you made such a lovely lure, dear goddess." Loki winked at her. "I never let you be bound to any dastardly giants, did I?"

"A little less bragging about past exploits and a little more finding our way out of this mess?" Hod suggested.

"I don't see why we can't do both. Why, look, this is a spitting image of my own hall, and—"

Loki's voice cut off with a muffled yelp. He looked down at the marble tile he'd just stubbed his toe on. A crack ran down the middle of it, one side raised higher than the other. The trickster's eyebrows drew together as he knit his brow.

A deeper shiver ran through me. When Loki let his concern show, you knew something was really wrong. "What is it?" I said.

"This cracked stone." He prodded the marble edge as we all came to a stop around him. "It plagued me for ages... until one of the craftsmen finally replaced it. The cracked one hasn't been there in at least a century."

"In the real Asgard," Thor said.

Baldur turned, his dreamy gaze focusing a little more closely on our surroundings. "I hadn't thought about it," he said in his melodic voice, "but that tall pine at the edge of the orchard—it was cut down not long before we left for Midgard last time."

I shifted my weight from one foot to the other. "What does that *mean*?"

Hod's expression had gone slack with understanding. "This Asgard isn't an exact replica of the current realm. It has bits and pieces from different times. Features we were more likely to remember even after they changed?"

"The memories that stood out the most," Loki said with a nod. "And who do we know who deals in memories?"

Freya's fingers tightened around the sword hilt. "The raven."

Loki's eyes lit with a frenetic gleam. "It all makes sense. How convincing this place is—how convincing that Odin was. How we were all fooled except for Ari." He nodded to me. "You have no experience with any part of Asgard outside of Valhalla to draw on. No recollections of being in Odin's presence. So the illusion couldn't catch hold quite as well."

"Illusion?" I said. This place felt awfully solid to be just a hallucination or something.

Loki took a step ahead of us, weaving his hands through the air with a flourish. "An illusion constructed out of our memories. Muninn didn't just lead us into this prison. She created it."

2

Baldur

"You're trying to tell me that little raven built this entire place?" Thor said to Loki with a sweep of his arm.

I followed his gesture, taking in the false Asgard again. This time I breathed a little deeper, opened my senses to it a little more freely so I could pick up the emotions floating around me. Tension radiated off my companions, which was why I'd tamped down my sensitivity in the first place. But getting out of here was more important than avoiding some immediate discomfort.

"I'm saying that's what the evidence suggests," the trickster replied. "I've seen her do it before—conjure objects or scenes out of memories she's gathered. Odin had her show me things a few times that way. Never anything on close to this scale before..."

He shook his head in awed disbelief at our surroundings. "This must be taking all her energy and concentration to maintain. And she'll be feeding off the memories she's gleaning from our minds right now."

Memories. A dark quiver ran through my thoughts like a sliver of ice. The last thing I wanted to do was dwell in the past. If Loki was right... what else might Muninn conjure out of our histories?

I didn't let myself glance at Hod, but my twin was there at the edge of my vision, with a shadowy scowl. So many things we'd put to rest between us... and now the raven might stir them up all over again. I didn't want to think about how much more pain she could cause him as well.

Instead, I trained my attention on the buildings around us, the courtyard we'd left behind, the distant trees. The whole sprawling realm. If Muninn was creating this out of her mind, then perhaps I could reach *her* emotions through it. Catch some impression that would help us navigate her prison.

Now that I was paying more attention instead of shutting off the negative vibes around me, a faint current of prickling resentment touched me along with the breeze. An anxious twitch. If that was her, she wasn't feeling very happy at the moment either. If there was some way to connect with her, to appeal to whatever good nature she had, was there any chance that we could sway her actions?

None of the impressions gave me the slightest opening. I didn't know how to extend my hand to a place born out of a person. What could I say to her when I had no idea where that anxiety or resentment might come from?

When I brought my focus back to my companions, Aria was watching me, her gray eyes clouded with concern. "Did you sense anything from her?" she asked.

When we'd summoned our valkyrie from her death, my contribution had been to bestow her with the same sensitivity to people's inner life—what the valkyries in olden times would have used to decide which of the warriors on the battlefield deserved to ascend to Valhalla. But that talent wouldn't be as strong for her, and she didn't have much practice using it yet.

"I think so," I said. "Nothing very clear—nothing we can use."

"Why would Odin's raven have shut us away in some false realm?" Freya said. "Surely she wasn't... *helping* the dark elves in whatever they've done with him? If he's even with them at all."

"He is," Aria said. "Or at least he was. I felt his presence clearly from their realm when I first went looking for him."

"She's hardly Odin's raven anymore," Loki said. "I haven't seen her with him in at least a couple centuries. He never did say how they came to part ways. I'm developing the sneaking suspicion it wasn't the friendliest of leave-takings."

"But to turn completely against him, and all of us..." I couldn't imagine any being's loyalties shifting so completely.

Muninn and Huginn, her partner and the raven of thought, had been constant fixtures at my father's side for ages, expanding his wisdom with their own travels. They might have been birds in form, for all Muninn now seemed able to transform into a womanly shape, but their minds had been as deep and sharp as any lesser god's. What could possibly have happened to turn her into an enemy?

The question made me want to shutter my mind all over again, but I knew that wouldn't protect me from the darkness lurking here. Not when it was lurking all around us as well as inside me.

My hands clenched at my sides for a second before I forced them to release. I needed to be out of this false place. We all did. The uncomfortable possibilities were wearing at the fragile harmony we'd managed to keep for so long—and the hard-won harmony within my own mind. So many horrible uncertainties looming over us... How long could we all stay strong?

"We have to assume she was working with the dark elves," Hod said. My brother's mouth set in a grim line. "She led us astray in their caves—they were holding her false Odin. She couldn't have pulled that off unless they were in on the plan. And then she tricked us into coming into this prison where we can't stop whatever else they have planned."

"That still doesn't answer why she would throw her lot in with them," Thor grumbled. "She was the one who approached *you*, wasn't she?" He eyed Loki.

"She was," Loki said. "After we'd already determined the dark elves were involved and taken up the search. I'd expect she wanted to know how close we'd gotten and to steer us wrong if she could. She was allied with them before we ever encountered her."

Aria sucked in a breath. "That ambush in the school —she brought us to that town, saying she'd seen the dark elves' markings. Pretending she was helping us track them down. She led us right to the school. She was fighting with us against them, but I guess that was just for show. That was a fucking trap too. She arranged that attack with them."

My back stiffened remembering that battle, the blasts of light I'd used to fell our attackers, the blood spilling under Thor's hammer. The blows Hod had taken, so vicious he'd been left on his knees at the end. The dark elves had meant to kill us if they could that day.

Muninn didn't just want us imprisoned, then. She'd have happily seen us dead.

Loki tapped his forefinger against his lips. "An excellent observation, pixie. She tried to have us slaughtered, and when that didn't work and your insight helped us find the gate, she must have realized there was no more diverting us—unless she gave us what we were after."

"Odin," Hod said with a grimace.

"Or some semblance of him. Enough of one that we'd follow him into her prison." The trickster let out a huff, glancing around the place again. "It is a rather *boring* one once you get used to it. Nothing but stillness and a landscape we've seen a million times."

"Odin save us from whatever you'd find more interesting, Sly One," Freya said with a roll of her eyes.

"This might not be all there is to it," Hod muttered. "Who says she's done with us at this?"

"She'll have to be done with us if we break our way out," Aria said. She raised her chin, determination brightening her gaze.

I could feel the turmoil churning inside our valkyrie's mind without any effort at all: uncertainty at what this unfamiliar place might hold, a sharp pang of worry for the brother she'd left behind, frustration at feeling helpless. But she wasn't letting those emotions bury her. Watching her, I summoned my own resolve. I could hold steady too. Not just for me, but for her as well. We were the ones who'd brought her here, who'd promised her we'd keep her safe.

I couldn't let my fears for myself stop me from protecting this young woman who'd come into our lives like a burst of light and fire.

"Why don't we take a fuller lay of the land, like we already started to?" I said. "There may be clues we can find that will speed up our escape. There might even be others she's trapped here." We hadn't seen the other inhabitants of the real Asgard often in the last several centuries. So many of us had wandered off in various directions now that we had little to occupy ourselves with here, with the great war done. But to know it wasn't just the six of us here alone would set my mind a little more at ease.

"We'll have to be careful that anyone we meet is real and not conjured," Hod said.

"All the same, we may as well have a look." Thor strode forward toward his great hall just up ahead.

"Let's see how well she's constructed the inside of my home."

We followed him along the path. He flipped his hammer in his hand in a gesture that looked almost playful, but the light in his eyes was fierce. The Thunderer didn't take well to being caged.

The sky overhead shone clear and blue, but with a false perfection that pressed down on me. My gaze slipped across the city toward the square contained deeper along its paths. The square where—

I clamped down on those thoughts before they could become fully conscious. A chill shuddered through my body all the same. Those were the last memories I wanted the raven scooping up and putting to her use.

The past was the past. It didn't matter anymore. It *shouldn't*.

Aria had fallen into step beside me. She glanced up at the shudder I hadn't quite contained. "Baldur?" she said softly.

The concern in her voice, despite all the fears she was facing herself, squeezed my heart.

"We'll get out," I said, as much for myself as for her. "Nothing's ever been able to trap the gods permanently yet."

She gave me that look as if she were trying to sense my own emotions, the ones stirring farther under the surface. The look that made some part of me tense and giddy at the same time, both reveling in her attention and fleeing it. It might be a wonderful thing to be known by a woman with a spirit like hers, but I kept certain things locked away for a reason.

I didn't ever want her to regret knowing me. That consideration came first.

She slipped her hand around mine, almost hesitantly, as if she thought I might pull away. The contact sent a warm tingle up my arm. I'd touched her before—to heal her wounds, mostly—but this overture felt more personal, more intimate. I gently twined my fingers with hers, and her smile, crooked but brilliant, almost made me forget where we were.

Then she raised her voice, sweet even if it was a bit thin, and started to sing.

It was one of the Beatles songs we'd played together a few days ago, her lending vocals to my guitar. A steady melody to match the resolute march of our feet. The lyrics were mostly nonsense, but the rhythm buoyed my spirits the way music always did. I couldn't lose myself in this, but I could wrap the tune around me like a shield.

I let my own voice roll out to join hers. Loki glanced back at us with an amused smirk. Hod shook his head, but a hint of a smile touched his lips. For a few minutes, our singing filled the empty space around us, as if to tell Muninn that no matter where she'd taken us, no matter what she had in store, we would not be shaken.

We ran out of lyrics just as we reached the door to Thor's hall. The thunder god shoved it open, and we all trailed in behind him, Aria and I at the back of the group. Her thumb skimmed the side of my hand, and suddenly I was thinking of how good it might feel if it traveled farther. If I took her right into my arms and lost myself in her brilliant defiance.

"I actually feel better now," she said with a halting

laugh. "Too bad you don't have all your instruments here."

"I'd rather listen to your voice anyway," I said honestly.

Her cheeks turned faintly pink. She gripped my hand tighter—and then dropped it at something she saw through one of the arched stone doorways in the hall. She spoke louder to address all of us. "Hey—do you think it's safe to stop for lunch?"

Thor's grand dining table was laid with bread and cheese and steaming drumsticks, jugs of mead and bowls of fruit. My mouth watered as the scents filled my nose. Odd that I hadn't noticed the smell until just a minute ago. That fact made my steps slow.

Thor advanced right up to the table and set down his hands on its end with a thud. "One way to find out," he said. "The raven had better not be spoiling my reputation for hospitality."

"Nephew," Loki said with a note of exasperation, but the thunder god had already snatched up one of the drumsticks.

He raised it to his mouth, and the second his teeth touched it, ready to tear into the gleaming flesh, the meat and bone disintegrated the way my father had in the courtyard. One second solid, the next a pile of dust. Thor grimaced and wiped his streaked fingers on his shirt.

Aria's face had fallen. She scooped a plum out of the fruit bowl, turned it in her hand, and tried it. It crumbled against her lips as the drumstick had.

"Not much of a lunch to be had here," Loki said.

Aria swiped her hand across her mouth. The tension

she'd found a brief release from had tightened her features again.

"Does that mean all the food in this place is garbage?" she said. "There's nothing at all here to eat?"

I hadn't felt all that hungry before, but at that question, a jab shot through my gut.

Had Muninn sent us here not just to stop us from finding Odin, but to starve us as well? The violent death she'd tried to arrange for us hadn't worked. This one would come on slower... but we couldn't fight our way out of it.

3

Aria

The ashy texture stayed on my fingers even after I tried to rub it off. My stomach hadn't twinged until I'd seen the food, but now it had tied into a huge knot. If Muninn hadn't conjured a single thing we could actually eat, we wouldn't last long in this place, would we?

The alarm that had been blaring in my head since we'd first realized this wasn't Asgard, that had only quieted momentarily when I'd distracted myself singing with Baldur, rang through my nerves again. I spun around, itching to release my wings, as if they'd help anything.

"Is anyone here?" I asked Thor.

He shook his head from where he was standing in the doorway. I'd seen his broad face both jovial and ferocious, but the morose look he had on now was something new.

A few dark auburn strands had slipped free from his short ponytail. They shifted against his square jaw as he worked it.

"We'll figure out something. We'll get out of here before it matters, Ari," he said.

Something about the way he said my name made me wonder if I was the one who had to worry the most. The gods had at least some immortality on their side. Thor could put away a whole roast cow in one sitting, I'd bet, but how often did they *need* to eat?

Probably a lot less often than I did.

The itching dug deeper. A way out. We had to get *out*.

My mind leapt to the only place in the real Asgard I'd ever seen: the inside of Odin's abandoned hall of warriors, Valhalla. At the back of its huge hearth lay a doorway that lead onto the branching path of Yggdrasil, the tree that connected Asgard to all the other realms. A thin hope wound through my chest. I grasped onto it.

"What about Yggdrasil?" I said. "We should see what Muninn's done with that, right? Maybe there's some way we can use it, or your memories of it, to leave."

"It might be overly optimistic to anticipate a loophole that large," Loki said, "but it can't hurt to take a look. All part of the grand tour."

He said it with his usual flippant tone and a flash of a grin, but he hung back to wait for me as the others headed down the hall. His hand came to rest lightly on my back between my shoulder blades, as if he knew the itch I was feeling.

Loki's touch could be hot enough to spark flames

under my skin—I'd gotten to experience that sensation to great effect a few mornings ago when we'd ended up in bed together—but he knew how to be careful too. The gentleness in that brush of his fingertips managed to heat me up anyway.

In theory, that hook-up had been a casual one-time thing. In practice... if I didn't die of starvation in here, I wasn't sure I was going to be able to stop myself from going back for seconds. The trickster had already made it clear he was up for another round.

I just had to remember that no matter how appealing his company could be, he *was* also a trickster. I got the impression none of the other gods trusted him completely, and they'd known him a lot longer than I had.

We hustled back across the courtyard we'd arrived in to the gilded hall at the other side. Stepping through Valhalla's broad doors, I felt abruptly more grounded, more present, than I had before.

Because Muninn had been able to draw on my memories as well as those of the gods when constructing the inside. The vacant tables, the spears and swords hung on the walls, the glitter of gold all around, the lingering smell of mead—it was all the way I'd seen it when I'd first arrived here using my valkyrie powers. If I'd been a proper valkyrie, back in the old days, I guessed this would have been my home.

Everything was the same, including the huge golden throne at the far end of the hall and the gaping fireplace beside it. I jogged past the tables to that and came to a halt.

There was no door in the back of the hearth the way

there should have been. Not even the faintest hint of one. I ducked and crunched over the strewn coals anyway to shove at the scorched stone back, but the bricks didn't budge.

"She didn't even want to pretend to leave a way open," Hod said. "I wonder if we could have made use of it if she had."

"Move, Ari," Thor said, his voice lower than usual. I clambered out and stepped back against one of the wooden benches.

"We don't need a doorway to get through." The thunder god's brown eyes flashed. His lips pulling back over clenched teeth, he heaved his arm and hurled his hammer at the fireplace.

Mjolnir slammed into the stones. They shattered with an ear-splitting crash. The hammer rebounded into Thor's hand, its metal surface gleaming. My heart leapt at the sight of the gaping blackness beyond the hole he'd broken open—for the two seconds before the stones jumped from the floor of the hearth and smoothed back into place.

"Damn it!" Thor growled out a few more curses in a language that wasn't English and whipped Mjolnir forward with so much force my hair fluttered in the stirred breeze. The entire hearth burst in a shower of clattering stone shards. They jittered on the floor as soon as they'd hit it and sprang back up before the hammer's handle had even found Thor's palm.

Thor whirled around. "Muninn!" he bellowed. "Come and face us! This is a coward's war you're waging." He flung the hammer at the tables. They smashed with a rain of splinters and melded back into place just as the hearth had. A growl escaped Thor's throat. He hauled his hammer arm back again, the red flush of battle rage spreading from his cheeks down his neck.

"Don't," I said, even though my chest had clenched in sympathy. There were a lot of things I'd have liked to smash right now too. "Don't let her goad you into wasting energy."

"Don't tell me what I can't do," Thor roared, spinning toward me.

I flinched at the fury in his voice, the wildness in his eyes—and his expression immediately faltered. His arm came down, the hammer dangling at his side. The fiery rage faded from his eyes as they softened.

"Ari. I'm sorry. I didn't—"

"It's okay," I said. I knew he hadn't planned to attack me. His regret at that brief outburst showed as clearly as it had when he'd blocked one of my strikes a little too hard in our sparring. I forced my fingers to unclench from the side of the bench where they'd clamped themselves and stepped toward him. "We're all frustrated. But obviously I was wrong. There's no way out in here."

He looked down at the hammer. "If I could just..."

Loki squeezed the broader god's shoulder. "I'm afraid we're not going to batter our way out of this one, old friend. At least not quite like that."

Thor made a vague grumbling sound. There was still something haunted in his gaze when he met my eyes again.

I pushed myself forward toward the entrance. "Let's

go, then. If that didn't work, then we try something else."
As long as we kept trying, then I didn't have to think
about what would happen if nothing worked.

The sun, if it even was the real sun, beamed down on
us as we came out of the hall. Freya shielded her eyes,
peering up at it. The vast sky didn't hold a single cloud.

"A prison without a ceiling," she said. "And all of us
with the power to propel ourselves into flight. That seems
a careless choice, don't you think?"

Loki's sly grin returned. "Shall we test the boundaries
of this Asgard?"

"Not all of us," she suggested. "But those who come
to flying most naturally?"

She tugged her falcon cloak from the folds of her
dress and flung it around her shoulders, contracting into
the shape of a bird of prey as it hit her skin. Loki hopped
into the air and glanced back at me.

"Are you coming, pixie?"

I hunched my shoulders, and my wings sprouted
with the usual prickly burning through my back. The
racerback tank I'd chosen exactly for that reason gave
them free rein to unfurl. The silver-white feathers glinted
at the edges of my vision.

A week or two ago, the weight of those appendages
on my wiry frame had felt oppressive. Now, with a single
flap and the rush of air over them, they sent a giddy
tremor through me. They gave me more freedom, not
less. Even if they also represented what I was now and
therefore all the things I'd lost to become a valkyrie. My
life, to begin with. A future in the world of fellow human
beings. Petey.

No, I wasn't thinking about that now. I hadn't completely lost Petey, not unless I let Muninn and her prison win.

Loki loped up toward the sky, heading toward the high walls he'd said his wager had helped build. Freya-as-falcon swooped after him. I sprang into the air, and my wings swept me on upward. The cooler wind buffeted my face when I turned it toward the sun.

Maybe it could be this simple. Just fly out into whatever realm Muninn had constructed her cage of memories in. Shatter the illusion by breaking through its outer limits.

I soared higher, as if I could dive into the fathomless blue overhead like an ocean. The wind washed over me with the smells of metal and stone and the apple orchard to the south and... a faint aftertaste of ash that lingered on my tongue.

Ash?

Before I could wonder much about that, Loki gave a shout. The trickster had stopped against what looked like the open expanse of the sky. But as I drew up beside him with a few more flaps of my wings, I felt it too. An invisible pressure holding us down.

I strained my wings, but I couldn't propel myself any higher. Scowling at the air above us, I swung a punch at it. The impact sent a spear of pain radiating down my arm as if I'd hit my funny bone hard.

Okay, not doing that again.

Freya's falcon was circling beside us, unable to go any higher either. "Not that I have much hope," Loki said, and beckoned me to follow him gliding farther across the city. Here and there, we tried to fly higher, only to be pressed back down. My skin started to crawl at the sensation of that vague unseen ceiling.

We really were trapped in here, as utterly as we could be.

I gritted my teeth against my nerves. My gaze slid down, skimming across the town. Before my eyes, the buildings, the courtyard, the square closer to the orchard —they all wavered. Just for an instant, as if something darker had rippled through them.

My body froze except for the sweep of my wings keeping me aloft.

"Did you see that?" I said.

Loki tipped his head to one side. "See what?"

"Asgard." I motioned to the city. "For a second, it was like something flickered past the illusion. Maybe the place we really are?"

Loki considered the ground below. His eyes narrowed. "I've got the sharpest eyesight of all of us, and nothing like that has caught my attention." His gaze came back to me. "You don't have solid memories of the city to make the illusion completely real to you. Just like you didn't with Odin. You may be our key to finding our way through this prison, pixie."

Wonderful. Five divine beings around me, and *I* was the one who held the key. "No pressure or anything, right?"

He chuckled and held out his hand. "I think we can at least say the sky is not our escape route. Let's rejoin the others."

Freya darted down with us as we descended. Thor,

Hod, and Baldur were waiting in the courtyard near the fountain. The goddess flew straight to join them, but Loki brought us down to earth at the edge of the marble-tiled space.

My feet hit the ground, and I willed my wings back into my body. I might take a weird sort of comfort in them now, but what I'd said to Thor about conserving energy applied to all of us.

"Ari," Loki said, and I turned. "Do you remember why I called you a pixie when we first met?"

I raised my eyebrows at him. "Because I'm small and I've got wings?"

He grinned. "Well, there's that, and there's also that pixies have more fight in every bit of their little bodies than any other being I've ever met. You don't want to tangle with a pixie. And you've already proven that no one should want to tangle with you."

He brushed his lithe fingers over my hair, sending a pleasurable shiver through me despite the tension balled in my stomach. When his head dipped, mine tilted automatically to meet his kiss. In the moment when his lips found mine, his fiery heat coursing over me, my nerves rang with all the power my new body contained, the power he and the other gods had given me. I didn't care that they might be watching. If anything happened between me and any of the others—and I'd already shared a kiss with Hod—it wasn't going to be under the pretense that they were my one and only.

Loki didn't linger in the kiss. He pulled back with a smaller smile that felt more private, more personal somehow. Then he swiveled toward the others with a graceful sweep of his arm. "No blasting out, no blasting off, but I think we may have the kernel of our answer. If we simply—"

I caught a flash of darkness at the corner of my vision. My head snapped around.

With a chorus of snarls, a pack of enormous monstrous wolves lunged across the courtyard's marble tiles toward us.

4

Aria

The nearest wolfish creature slammed into me before I had time to react, shoving me away from Loki and pinning me to the ground with a gnash of teeth and a scraping of claws. The smack of my spine against the hard tiles shocked a cry from my throat. Pain seared across my chest with the slash of its claws.

I lashed out with all my god-given strength, ramming a knee into the beast's gut, whacking my forearm as hard as I could into its throat. Spittle dribbled onto me as its jaws lunged closer. I punched it in the muzzle. A sputter of the lightning I'd been able to intermittently summon sparked from my hand.

The monster flinched, relaxing its hold just long enough for me to heave it off me and scramble away. Blood dribbled down my shirt from where its claws had raked across my collarbone. The burn of that wound faded away behind the rush of adrenalin and the thudding of my pulse.

Wargs. That was what the gods called these over-sized, overly vicious wolves that held an almost human intelligence in their yellow eyes. I'd tangled with three of them in an abandoned factory yard a week ago, a battle that had ended with my first real kill and left me shaken. It might be my memory Muninn had stolen the creatures from.

Stolen them and multiplied them. As I urged my wings to release from my back and yanked my switchblade from my jeans pocket, I counted ten wargs facing off against me and my godly companions. Freya was swinging her sword at one's snapping jaws, Hod tangling another with thick strands of shadow. Baldur blasted one back with a surge of light he propelled from his hands. Loki flung a ball of fire into the face of another while Thor barged into the pack's midst with a roar, his hammer cracking ribs here, a skull there.

When Mjolnir bashed the one warg's skull, the creature didn't simply fall. It crumbled into dust like so many things in this fake Asgard.

I lifted off the ground with a sweep of my wings, just in time to escape the snap of the warg that had already tackled me once. It growled and tried to leap after me. The dust of the one Thor had killed didn't rise again like the rubble of the fireplace or the splinters of Valhalla's table. I guessed the raven woman didn't have enough power to keep illusions that acted like living, moving beings going forever.

The warg sprang at me again, its glinting claws

swiping just below my feet. If it'd been a real living being, I would have felt the stirring of its life energy inside its body. I'd have been able to open up the shadows inside my valkyrie body and claim that life like valkyries once did as they decided the winners and losers on a battlefield. But the monster beneath me radiated nothing but hollowness. Just a construct, like Loki had said. A puppet, with Muninn pulling the strings somewhere hidden.

A puppet that had left me battered and bleeding. I gritted my teeth and dove. It wasn't really alive, so I didn't need to feel the slightest twinge of conscience over slaughtering it.

The warg twisted around, but I was too fast. I stabbed my blade straight down into the top of its head. A choked whine broke from its mouth, and then it was disintegrating like its companion.

I whipped my knife hand up and whirled around. Another warg was barreling toward me. I dodged, not quite fast enough to escape its maw. Its teeth sank into the edge of my wing and tore. That pain seared sharp through my nerves. I gasped as I wrenched my wing free.

I aimed a kick at the monster, slamming my heel into its cheek. The monster reeled to the side, right into the fiery slash of Loki's dagger. He wrenched the curved blade deeper into the creature's chest, and it crumpled into another heap of dust.

The trickster wiped his hands with a grimace and raised his head. The polished tiles of the courtyard were strewn with more piles of dust. Freya was just lifting her sword from the warg she must have taken down, sweat-damp tendrils of hair clinging to the sides of her smooth face. Thor walloped the last of the pack with his hammer, sending the beast skidding into the base of the fountain, where it crumbled too.

We stood there in the stillness, no sound but the rasp of our breaths, waiting to see if the battle was really over. Thor glanced at me and made a strangled sound. He strode over, his gaze fixed on the gashes across my collarbone.

"The raven is going to pay for that," he growled.

Now that the rush from the fight was fading, the throbbing of the wounds prickled deeper. I clenched my jaw against the pain. Baldur came up beside Thor, and I stepped toward him, knowing what he was offering without him needing to say a word. He'd healed my wounds enough times in the last couple weeks. It was basically becoming a hobby for him.

The god of light gave me a soft smile and laid his hand over the wounds. His power washed over me with a flood of warmth and an itchy tingling where the skin was knitting back together. When he lowered his arm, nothing remained of the cuts except dark pink lines like scars, but even those would fade in a few days. Unfortunately, I'd had to learn that from experience.

The neckline of my tank top was ripped, and the white fabric streaked with blood. Not much I could do about that without a convenient wardrobe on hand. I wet my lips. Construct or not, that thing could have killed me if I'd reacted any slower, if it'd caught my stomach instead of my chest. It looked like the raven woman wasn't content to just let me starve to death.

The wargs had attacked us right after I'd told Loki I'd seen her illusion waver. Right after he'd reminded me that I could be a real threat. My fingers tightened around the handle of my switchblade.

My older brother Francis had given me that weapon when I was just a kid, to protect myself against the monsters in our life back then—the ones in human form. Back then, I'd failed to protect myself with it. I'd failed to protect him when maybe I could have saved his life.

I wasn't going to fail the gods who'd given *me* a new life. I sure as hell wasn't going to fail Petey. I'd promised to be there for him, whether he remembered that promise or not. If the raven thought she was going to break me, she had another thing coming.

"Muninn!" I shouted, swiveling to take in the city beyond the courtyard. "Stealing from my head now? What else did you see? What exactly have I done to deserve the way you're trying to beat us down here, huh? I've never hurt anyone except people already trying to hurt me. What's your excuse, you asshole?"

"Ari," Baldur said softly, but I ignored him. This wasn't the right time for peace-making.

We needed to tear her down. Was there any way to weaken her concentration? If I could shake her, that might shake the whole illusion around us. Open up a way for us to escape.

I pictured the woman I'd met when she'd approached Loki and me offering her help. Slim with big dark eyes and mussed but glossy black hair. The little bird-ish quirks she kept even in human form, in the cock of her head and the slight hoarseness to her voice. What would rattle her? She hadn't cared about Thor calling her a coward. But she'd once been the Allfather's constant companion while he oversaw all of Asgard—the real thing. She'd flown through every realm, gathering memories from all over.

"Is this all you do now?" I called out, turning again. "Rule over a little jail for six people? No time to stretch your wings, to pay attention to anything else. Who put you up to this—the dark elves? Why did you let them stick you with such a shitty job?"

Loki sounded as if he'd smothered a chuckle. And a dark flicker caught my eye near the hall opposite Valhalla. A movement like the flap of a wing.

My pulse stuttered with a sudden certainty. She was here. She was right in here with us, lurking behind her constructs. She probably had to be to keep them going—close enough to steal the memories she needed from our heads.

I jogged up the path to the hall, scanning the stone walls, the thatched roof, the solid oak door. "You know I'm right. I bet you can see that too. I don't know what happened between you and Odin, why you're doing this, but you *know* it has nothing to do with me. This is just cruelty. Are you a monster like those wargs you sent at us, Muninn? Are you—"

Another flash of dark feathers shimmered against the pale stones. I threw myself toward it. My hand closed around nothing but air. Then, with a creaking groan, the entire front wall of the building tipped toward me.

I stumbled backward with a yelp, throwing up my

arms. The wings I hadn't retracted yet arced over me too. They might have been the only thing that saved me.

The stones pummeled me, and I fell to my hands and knees. The feathered appendages protruding from my back took the worst of the battering. An ache spread through them, but my more fragile head and ribs just pressed against the ground, unbashed.

"Ari!" someone shouted. There was a grunt and a thud as Thor must have started clearing the rubble. I tested my wings against the stones that had buried them and winced.

One of those stones was heaved off me, and I managed to shove another to the side. My wings retracted with a pained tremor. I kicked at the rocks on my legs.

An arm wrapped around my shoulders, helping to tug me free from the rest of the rubble. Hod's arm. I crawled out into the press of his embrace, the salty and faintly smoky smell of him surrounding me.

"I'm okay," I mumbled against his shirt.

He let out a shaky laugh. "Half of a damned building just fell on you, valkyrie, and that's all you've got to say for yourself?" He pulled back, his blind gaze managing to settle on mine as if he were looking back at me, his fingers tracing down the sides of my face. My breath hitched when his thumb brushed a scrape on my cheek. His jaw clenched. "You *are* hurt."

"I've been worse," I said. "Next time she'll have to try throwing the whole building at me." When his expression didn't shift, I added, "You want to kiss it better?"

"Ari," he muttered, but the glimmer that lit in his eyes and the sudden flush of heat between us suggested that yeah, maybe he did. And I would have been perfectly okay with that. But he straightened up instead, helping me to my feet with him. The others had gathered around us. I suspected Hod wasn't quite the exhibitionist Loki liked to be.

The trickster gave us an amused look, but there was a serious note in his jaunty voice. "What was that about, pixie? Did you see something else we couldn't? Because whatever happened there, the raven obviously wasn't pleased with you."

"I saw *her*," I said, brushing grit from my arms. My legs felt a bit wobbly, but my valkyrie strength was already steadying me despite the various bruises forming on my limbs. "She's here with us. Listening to everything we say." I raised my chin. "Which means she can get to us, but it should also mean we can get to her."

5

Hod

I stepped away from the rubble of the collapsed hall—one that in the real Asgard had been Bragi's, if my mental map of the city hadn't failed me—and almost tripped over a chunk of stone. I'd rushed toward the crash and Ari's cry so quickly I hadn't taken the time to chart out the lay of the land with the senses I did have at my disposal. Now it was a maze of uncertain obstructions. It was a miracle I'd managed to make it to her without falling on my face in the first place.

Ari's hand caught mine, though I'd already found my balance. I couldn't say I minded the warmth of her fingers curling around mine, but at the same time the reason she'd reached for me sent a wash of shame through me.

We were the gods here. We should be shielding her, not the other way around.

I should at least manage to stay on my feet without her help.

I squeezed her hand, letting myself revel for a few moments in the gentle strength of her grip, and let go. Not without a pang of loss, even though she was still right beside me.

There was something developing between us, something we hadn't had much chance to talk about what with the battle with the dark elves and now this. I wasn't sure I'd want to tell her just how much I hoped it *could* be just yet. She'd been happy for a little time with me, when we'd sat together and kissed as she'd steeled herself to leave her brother behind. She deserved to be happy. I never wanted anything I felt to turn into another burden for her.

"Hmm," Loki was saying. I stiffened automatically at the mischief in his tone. You never knew what schemes the trickster was going to come up with when he started sounding like that. His clothes rustled as he swung around. "I think I'd like to take a look at the site of our missing bridge."

"What, you think *you're* going to summon it now?" I said, testing my feet against the ground. Another hunk of stone lay to my left. Pebbles scattered under the sole of my right shoe. "Even if this isn't the real Asgard, I doubt Muninn is going to let you play Allfather." As much as Loki would probably enjoy lording that role over all of us.

"I may have a plan," he said in his sly way. Not telling us what that plan *was*, of course. That would spoil his bizarre version of fun. "Come on. We'll all want to be ready if it works."

Feet rasped against the ground as the others moved to follow him. My body balked. "Ari saw the raven *here*. Don't you think we should investigate that sighting first?"

"I'm not sure you're the best person to be making decisions based on sight, dear nephew," Loki called what sounded like over his shoulder.

My teeth gritted. Before I could snap out another retort, Ari leaned closer to me, a warmth and a whiff of her sweetly sharp scent. "Let's just see what he's got in mind," she said. "I doubt Muninn stuck around here after she tossed that wall on me anyway. I know you and Loki don't really get along, but from the stories I keep hearing, it sounds like he is pretty good at figuring his way out of sticky situations."

"He is, when it suits him," I muttered, but I started to move. After a couple steps, I stubbed my toe on another errant stone and winced.

"Do you want me to—" Ari started.

"No," I said quickly, before she could offer to act as guide. I'd lived in Asgard for centuries upon centuries, even if it'd been a while since I'd been back there. I wasn't going to be led around this facsimile of my home like an invalid.

I summoned a swath of shadow to me, forming it into a narrow chilly length in my hands. Like a cane. Still not ideal, still not how I wanted our valkyrie seeing me—this reminder of what I lacked—but at least it would let me avoid any further obstacles Muninn threw in our path without assistance.

The others' footsteps had already moved away from us. I swept the cane of shadows over the ground as I strode after them, stepping around the rubble it caught on. The breeze was washing away the dust of the collapse, leaving only the crisp meadow-like smell that was far too much like my real home.

Because the raven had stolen it out of my memories of home, of course.

"So, you can see more than the others?" I said to Ari, still a warm whisper of fabric beside me. "Past Muninn's construction?"

"Just a little so far, here and there," she said. "When she's distracted, maybe? I haven't figured out a definite pattern, but that was what I was trying to do back there. To break her focus and see if I could get another glimpse."

"Don't ignore your other senses, then," I said. "Listen, smell, taste, touch... She's using them all to build this place, but that means every aspect can falter. We need all the clues we can get."

"You're right. I wasn't even thinking of that." She paused. "Have you smelled anything that's kind of ashy? Or is that something you'd expect to smell around here that maybe the others would be remembering?"

Ash in Asgard? "There might sometimes have been a bit of wood-smoke scent in the air from the hearths," I said. "Not often while it was warm like this, though."

She brushed her hair back from her face with a rustle of those soft waves. "Not wood-smoke. There's something a little more... chemical-y to it? That's why it didn't seem to fit. But I've only noticed it once, and then it faded. I don't know if it means anything."

"We'll have to keep it in mind," I said. "Unless the

great Loki has already solved all our problems and we're about to walk right out of here."

"You never know," Ari said, but her tone was teasing. She fell silent for a moment, her shoes tapping against the smooth marble stones. "Do you two just get on each other's nerves, or is there a bunch of history I don't know there?"

"History," I said. "A lot of it." Not any I wanted to think about, even though it was hanging over me with every second we spent in this place. Normally Asgard didn't make me think about those times unless I let my mind go there, but with the city turned into a prison, it was hard to avoid the most negative associations.

"More tragedies you don't want to share with me yet?" Ari prodded. She kept her voice gentle, but she couldn't completely disguise the note of disappointment. She'd ended up sharing an awful lot of her painful history with me in the last week. The things she'd been through... I shuddered to remember them in the little detail she'd offered. It'd been easy enough to fill in the blanks.

I wished I could show her the same vulnerability in turn, but I wasn't solely the victim in my history. The parts that closed my throat and weighed down my tongue were laced with guilt.

Would she talk to me like this, touch me like she had a moment ago, if she knew the whole story? I wasn't sure it cast me in that much a better light than it did Loki. I'd prefer it if I never had to find out.

"It's long and complicated," I said. "And I don't think getting into it would be very productive toward getting out of here. It's just hard not to be reminded."

"Well, I don't know what happened, but you've stuck it out with him this long. Maybe you can cut Loki a little slack at least until we are out of here?" She bumped her elbow gently against mine.

It was hard to argue with that. Not that I'd wanted to spend all my days since Ragnarok with the Sly One around, but he and the Allfather had their seemingly unshakeable bond that I'd never understood, and Thor considered him an ideal partner for adventuring more than an annoyance most of the time, so by falling in with them, Baldur and I had fallen in with Loki too.

If he was so sly, so clever, why hadn't the trickster spotted *this* trick before it'd trapped us? I'd like to hear him explain that.

But because Ari had asked me to, I held my tongue as we joined the others where they'd stopped at the far end of the courtyard, where the rainbow bridge had set us down. I might not have ever seen the gleaming colors others had described to me in the past, but when it was here, its magic gave off a faint vibration, left a taste like sugary sap in the air. I discerned nothing of it now. The bridge had disappeared the moment we'd stepped off it with the false Odin.

I sensed Baldur's presence near me, like the warmth of sunlight on skin. I shifted a little closer. My twin had at least as many horrible memories that could be dredged up here as I did, and in them he was definitely a victim. He'd retreated so far into that dreamily peaceful state since we'd come back after Ragnarok, as if living in that haze was the only thing that let him keep the harmony he was always chasing. How long could he hold onto it here, shoved so far out of his comfort zone?

Norns willing, we'd never have to find out.

"How are you holding up?" I asked him quietly.

"Well enough," he said serenely, but I thought I heard a slight stiffness in his voice that wasn't usually there. "Hopeful that whatever experiment the trickster has thought up will get us somewhere."

Ahead of us, Loki clapped his hands. "Oh, Muninn!" he called out in a singsong voice. "You can hear me, can't you? Our little raven voyeur. Take a little trip with me, will you?"

What in Hel's name was the trickster up to? I shifted on my feet, drinking in the air, taking in the sounds of the false realm around us.

Loki's voice carried on, at a steady lulling pace, almost hypnotizing. "Think of all those times you crossed Bifrost with Odin. Perched on his cloaked shoulder or soaring in the air beside him. His feet thumping across that shimmering surface. The colors blazing beneath you, red and yellow and blue and everything between. The clouds parting into mist that tickled against your feathers. The green sprawl of Midgard's lands spreading out ahead of you."

A quiver crept over my skin. My breath caught. He was trying to draw the memory out of *her*, to cajole her into adding an exit to our prison by getting her to focus on the bridge. And it was working. The air vibrated with more power, an echo of the rainbow bridge's magic. Was it starting to form before the others' eyes even now? Ari stirred beside me as if in anticipation.

"Maybe Heimdall was there to offer you a wave and a few words in that gravelly voice, in that watchtower of his poised on Asgard's edge," Loki went on. "Or maybe it was just you and your partner in flight and your master, climbing that brilliant arc and—"

The quiver of magic snapped away in an instant, like a door slamming shut. A fierce wind blasted into us, sending us stumbling apart. It whirled around and wrenched me straight off the ground.

"No!" I shouted, but the wind ate my words too. It flung me through space I couldn't feel other than the lash of air against my skin and clothes, and threw me down on hard cold ground. As quickly as the wind had risen up, it slipped away, leaving me in silence.

Total silence. Not a voice, not a breath, not a rustle of clothing except my own. I swallowed, the sound of that action enormous in my ears. "Ari? Baldur? Thor?"

My voice rang out unanswered. Wherever the raven had tossed me, it was away from the others.

An edge of icy fear jabbed through my gut. If she'd done this to me, what had she done to my twin? To our valkyrie?

6

Aria

The world spun around me, the ground tipping. The marble slabs from the ground flew up between me and my companions. I tried to throw myself at a gap between them, and a burst of wind shoved me back.

I tipped head over heels and sprawled on the ground... which was not the ground anymore. My hands pressed against fine-grained wooden boards as I shoved myself upright. My heart lurched.

The courtyard we'd been standing in, the shimmer of the bridge starting to form, the gods and goddess I'd been standing with—they were all gone. But the place I'd found myself in wasn't exactly new. It was the only place in Asgard I'd been at all familiar with before today.

The gold, weapon-lined walls of Valhalla rose around me. A vacant bench stood at a thick oak table just a few feet from where I was sitting. The high ceiling glinted overhead. The cloying smell of alcohol and manly musk tickled my nose.

I scrambled all the way onto my feet. The wooden floor thumped under them as I jogged to the nearest side door between the mounted swords and spears. I gripped the handle and wrenched at it, but it didn't budge.

Shit. I pushed on to the next, and then next, all the way down to the broad door at the opposite end of the room from Odin's throne. When I reached it, my palms were stinging from heaving at so many. I still gave that one a good yank.

It didn't move an inch. The smack of my shoulder didn't move it either. I glared at it, rubbing the side of my arm.

Muninn had locked me in here, away from the gods. What had she done with them? And why had she put me here?

No, I didn't need to ask that. She'd tossed me into the place I had the clearest memories of so that she could build her construct on a stable foundation. All the better to trap me with. She didn't want there to be any chance that I'd see through this illusion to her or wherever we really were.

Voices echoed behind me. I spun around. At the sight that met me, I jerked backward, bracing myself against the door with a hiccup of my pulse.

The once-empty tables had filled with figures. Men in battle armor, metal or leather, muscles bulging as they grabbed mugs of mead or snatched hunks of meat off the roasts now sitting on platters between them. They packed every bench throughout the long hall. Here one rose his mug in a toast. There another threw back his head with a bellow of a laugh.

They weren't modern warriors. From their clothes, the ruddy tint to many of the heads of hair, the thick beards most of them were sporting, I had to guess these were Viking warriors from ancient times. The snippets of shouted conversation I caught were in a language I didn't know. They looked like they were having a good time, though. And the smell of the roasts made my mouth water.

That meat would probably disintegrate into dust if *I* tried to eat it, wouldn't it? These men, they were part of the illusion too. Not from my memories, but I guessed from that of the Asgardians here with me. Muninn obviously had no problem stitching constructs together from several different sources.

A figure in a white dress laid over with silver armor wove between two of the tables near me. A woman. My gaze followed her, startled. Her long blond hair tumbled down her back and her face was soft with youth, but muscles flexed in her own arms as she handed out more mugs to the assembled warriors.

There were others like her, more women in dressed-up armor, circulating through the room. A few wore battle helmets and most, I noticed, carried swords or daggers strapped to their belts. Warrior women.

Valkyries. A rush of understanding filled me. These were the original valkyries, the ones Odin had summoned way back when. The ones who'd flown into battle to harvest the souls of worthy men to bring them back here. I hadn't realized they'd acted as waitresses in between those times. I couldn't say I was sorry I'd missed that part of the gig.

I eased toward them, tensed to leap back if any of the conjured people showed any sign of aggression. But they kept eating and drinking and serving the tables as if I wasn't there. Gradually, my shoulders came down. I ambled down the aisles, glancing over the faces, trying to ignore the growing pang in my stomach.

Why had Muninn constructed all of them? They weren't trying to hurt me. She could have just left me in this place alone if she'd only wanted to imprison me. I didn't get it. But then, the raven woman had always seemed pretty kooky. Maybe this was for her entertainment.

A low, rolling chuckle carried from the head of the room, and my feet froze in place. Muninn had conjured one more figure. A tall, broad-shouldered man with a travel-worn cloak and a chestnut beard flecked with silver, one eye lost behind the gouge of a scar, was leaning back in the throne I'd only ever seen empty before.

Odin. I'd imagined him there when I'd first come to Valhalla on my own, a picture drawn by instinct. I'd thought I was walking across the bridge with him just a couple hours ago. But this... this wasn't the real Allfather, not any more than these were real warriors around me or this the real Valhalla, but he was as close to the real one as I'd gotten. Not a shuffling wounded puppet like the one who'd led us here. A vibrant reflection of the god from his actual life.

I edged closer, dodging a warrior who tipped back on his bench as he pounded the table in amusement. Odin's one light brown eye roved over the assembly. His lips were curled in a smile I could only call satisfied.

Two wolves sprawled on the floor by the foot of the throne. Not huge monstrous ones like the wargs, but regular sized, one gray and one black. Their ears stayed perked, but their heads rested languidly on their forepaws. Their gazes didn't twitch toward me either as I passed the last row of tables.

A raven perched on Odin's shoulder, its head bobbing as it leaned close to its master. Muninn or the other raven Loki had mentioned to her—of thought, he'd said? I couldn't remember that one's name.

If that was Muninn, was it the real one? Incorporating herself into this tableau while she spied on me?

My legs balked for a second. Then I marched right up to the throne and swiped my hand at Odin's shoulder.

My fingers collided with a feathered body. The raven squawked indignantly as I smacked it forward. With a ruffling of feathers, it hopped back to its perch. Odin didn't stir from his contemplation of his warriors.

All just part of the illusion, then. I frowned, following Odin's gaze over the crowded hall. Okay, I'd gotten to see the party. Now how the hell was I going to get out of here?

Somehow the throng of great warriors looked different from over here. Their faces seemed more shadowed. Before all the voices had sounded pleased or triumphant.

Now... Now an angry shout reached my ears. At a nearby table, one of the men had yanked another to his feet by the front of his shirt. The second man punched the first in the face, so hard blood spurted from the guy's nose.

In his throne beside me, Odin laughed. The sound rolled over me, setting the hairs on my arms on end.

Over there, some brawny guy had his face so deep in his mug he was practically snorkeling in his mead. When he raised his head, his cheeks were flushed. He swayed a little in his seat. He slammed his mug against the table and bellowed at a passing valkyrie to bring him more.

A platter clanged on the floor. A row of warriors on one bench jostled with each other as they fought over the choicest bits of meat on a goose they'd just been brought. Over here, a man grabbed a sword off the wall and jabbed it at one of his companions. They dodged back and forth in a dance of sword play, their blades clattering together. But they weren't just playing around. Their mouths twisted with hostility.

Even the gold on the walls looked tarnished now, dented here and there from a bash of a blade. One warrior flung another against the wall, and the building shuddered. A few golden flakes tumbled down from the ceiling like glittering snow.

"Bravo!" Odin called from his throne. "Let the feasting continue!" The set of his mouth looked uncomfortably like a smirk now.

Why had the scene changed? Had this really been what Valhalla was like back then? It didn't fit with what the other gods had told me. Why would the valkyries have brought back assholes instead of honorable warriors? Why would Odin have cheered them on when they squabbled? What would be the point of Valhalla if it was like this?

I paused, glancing at Odin's shoulders again. At the single raven on one, the other one bare.

Maybe these weren't memories from any of the gods. Muninn would have spent tons of time in this hall with Odin, wouldn't she? It'd be in her memories she was least likely to picture herself there rather than just what she'd seen around her.

And apparently what she'd seen had looked to her like a bunch of drunkards waging little wars against each other, with Odin egging them on. She clearly wasn't an Odin fan these days. It could be her memories had gotten skewed. Whatever the case, she'd wanted to show this to me. To give me her side of the story? Was this supposed to convince me that throwing us into this prison was justified?

"Are you trying to prove to me that Odin deserves whatever you're doing to him?" I called up toward the rafters. "It's a little hard to assume your take on things is unbiased. And he let all of these people go, didn't he? He sent off the warriors and the valkyries to finish their lives... after-lives... however they wanted. Even if you don't like how he ran the hall, he stopped it."

No answer. Not even a hint that she'd heard me.

The men having the fight by the wall spun around each other. The bigger one shoved the lankier one into the wall again. More gold flakes fluttered down. I traced their path backwards, up through the air toward the arched ceiling. A sliver of sunlight shone through the gold thatch.

An idea prickled through the back of my mind. Loki had been able to shift Muninn's thoughts enough to get her to picture the rainbow bridge, to bring it partly into being, and that was something she hadn't been meaning to think about at all. If I could work with the impressions she was already giving me, maybe I could trick her into giving me what I needed.

I flexed my shoulders, urging my valkyrie wings out from my back. They spread out on either side of me, heavy and solid. Mine. I flapped them to lift just a few feet off the ground.

"I get the picture," I said, pitching my voice over the din of the crowd. "Valhalla was a shitty place. The warriors were pricks. Odin was a bigger prick. The gold was dulling. The mead going sour. The ceiling starting to crumble."

I swept up a little higher, gliding over the warriors. More of them were fighting now, this one tossing mead in that one's face, another clambering right up on the table to kick at his neighbor's head. Real nice, guys. Keeping it classy. I'd known gangsters back in my first life whose company I'd have preferred.

Or were they just responding to Muninn's thoughts as she responded to what I was saying?

"Those weapons look ready to fall off the walls," I said. "I'm just waiting for one of those benches to crack right open. Odin would probably laugh at that, right? At least until that pretty throne of his toppled right over. Or will the roof fall in on his head? It's awfully wobbly. Barely holding together at all. He's lucky it hasn't already crashed down."

As I said the last few words, I shot up toward the ceiling with a few swift beats of my wings, as fast as they could carry me. At the last second, I spun backward and aimed my legs at the layers of golden straw with a massive kick.

My feet burst through the ceiling, so fragile in Muninn's mind. I flapped my wings and soared up through the hole I'd made, out toward the freedom of the bright blue sky with a gust of fresh air filling my lungs, and—

The walls below me toppled completely. A force walloped me from behind. I whirled, my head dizzy, and a sensation twanged faintly in my chest. From my heart.

One of the gods who'd made me—one of them was close. If I could just hold on to that feeling, maybe I could...

I focused all my attention on that pale tug. My body whipped around again, and I tumbled forward onto hard-packed earth.

7

Aria

I leapt back up, tensed and wary, my feet braced against the earth. I'd landed in a meadow, grass sprouting here and there from the dry ground, with a hall nearly as large as Valhalla in front of me. No gold on this one, though, just stone.

No one else was around. It was just me and the warm breeze and a whiff of apple blossoms from somewhere nearby. I guessed I hadn't managed to make it to the god I'd sensed after all. Where the hell had Muninn sent me now, and why?

Voices filtered through the hall's wide door. Hoots and laughter—and a pained shout. My wings snapped open from where they'd folded against my back in my fall. Before I could take a step toward the hall, the door burst open with so much force it smacked the stone wall beside its frame.

Loki bolted out, his hair flying back from his forehead in a pale red flame, his strides lengthening as his shoes of flight lifted him off the ground. Oh. I guessed I'd found my way in the right direction after all. I moved to hurry after him, and a horde of figures charged out of the hall.

These men weren't human warriors like in Valhalla. They might be constructs with no real life energy for me to sense, but something about their bearing, the power in their movements, told me they were gods.

Loki was already outpacing them. Then a shining silver shape whipped through their midst and slammed into his back. With a gasped curse, he toppled to the ground.

The silver shape flew back into the hall. I froze for a second, staring. Had that been *Thor's* hammer? Why would he be attacking Loki? Or was that just what Muninn wanted me to think?

The mass of other gods descended on the fallen trickster. "You're not getting out of this, Sly One," a swarthy man growled. Another yanked Loki's arms behind his back at an angle that made Loki wince. His eyes blazed. He managed to kick one god in the gut and another in the groin before one of them heaved up his legs too.

"Muninn!" Loki rasped out. "Once was fucking enough. When I get my hands on you, I'm going to wring that feathered neck until—"

Yet another god shoved his meaty hand over the trickster's mouth. They hauled him toward the hall.

No. My body lurched into action. I sprang into the

air, throwing myself at the closest of the gods tormenting the flailing Loki. "Let him go, you assholes! Let him *go!*"

My elbow jabbed the god in the eye while I aimed a kick at his ribs. He grunted, his hold loosening. I spun around to tackle the god beside him, and a huge fist connected with my temple.

I'd faced off against godly strength before, the times Thor and I had sparred while he was teaching me to use the strength and speed he'd given me. But he'd been holding back then, not really trying to hurt me. A valkyrie was no real match for a god. And this one hadn't held back at all.

Pain splintered through my skull. I reeled backward, my wings jerking, and landed in a heap on my hands and knees. My vision stuttered as I blinked. I shoved myself back to my feet, toward the throng. They were just constructs. I should be able to stop them. I couldn't just sit here while they manhandled Loki.

My head was still throbbing. I staggered before I found my balance.

"*Ari.*"

My legs locked at the urgency in Loki's ragged voice. My gaze found his through the crowd of gods around him. His mouth was free, but they held his arms and legs as tightly as before. He'd gone limp in his attackers' grasp. The blaze in his eyes had simmered down to a smolder that sent a twisting sensation through my gut.

I couldn't normally use the sensitivity to emotions that Baldur had given me all that well on the gods, but right now I barely needed it to read the trickster's expression. There was anger there still, but also resignation... and shame.

"Leave it," he said. "They'll be done with me soon. You might keep that switchblade of yours ready, though."

The gods marched back to the hall, carrying him between them. He stayed silent in their grasp as they pushed inside. The door thumped shut behind them.

What the hell was going on? Was *this* from someone's memories—Loki's, I'd have to guess? Or was Muninn stitching together bits and pieces into a horrible new scenario like she had with the wargs?

He'd wanted me to have my switchblade ready. I rubbed the tender spot on my temple where that god had punched me and pulled the knife from my pocket.

More bellows—some that sounded angry, and then others of amusement—carried through the building's door. I shifted my weight from one foot to the other, debating whether I should charge in there despite what Loki had said. He couldn't know exactly what Muninn had planned any more than I did. Although I wasn't sure there was any situation I could get him out of if he couldn't himself. It just didn't feel right to simply wait out whatever awful things they might be doing to him. They hadn't looked like they only wanted a polite chat.

I'd just gathered my resolve and started toward the hall when the door flew open again. Loki strode out, a wave of godly laughter ringing after him. I bristled, but none of the other gods appeared at the doorway.

The trickster was shadowing his mouth with one hand. He held the other out to me with a beckoning twitch of his fingers. His smoldering eyes didn't quite meet my gaze.

"What?" I said. "What did they do to you? Are you okay?"

He didn't speak, just made another twitching gesture with his fingers. Right, the switchblade. I frowned as I handed it over.

Loki's hand dipped for just an instant as he spun away from me, and I caught a glimpse of what he'd been trying to hide. Thick black lines zigzagged across his clamped lips, piercing the skin above and below with angry pink wounds. A choked sound escaped me.

Loki jerked the blade across his face. Bits of a black material that looked like leather rained down as he coughed and spat. The fragments disintegrated into dust when they hit the ground.

The trickster turned back to me, rubbing his mouth. I braced myself, but when he lowered his arm, his face looked the same as it always had. Because he'd healed already or because he'd shifted his features to hide the wounds? I'd seen him transform his face into that of a woman's before. I'd seen him morph into a wolf. He clearly didn't like that I'd seen him in this state at all.

He thrust the folded switchblade toward me. The second my fingers closed around it, he started walking. "Come on, let's get away from this wretched place."

I had to speed-walk to keep up with him. We skirted the hall and ventured into a thick stretch of forest, all pines and aspen, behind it. I contracted my wings to avoid the branches.

When the trees had closed in between us and the

hall, Loki's pace slowed. He still hadn't looked directly at me since he'd come out.

"What was that all about?" I said quietly. "They... They *sewed* your mouth shut. Muninn must have some kind of sick mind to—"

"Don't blame her for that part," Loki broke in in a sharply flippant tone. "Other than her role in recreating it. These are memories, pixie, remember? You're getting a real introduction to the world of the gods."

My stomach clenched. "Then that really happened. They really— Thor helped them, didn't he? That was his hammer that stopped you from getting away."

"We all do things we're not especially proud of when caught up in the fervor of a crowd, hmm?"

"But *why*? Why would they do that to anyone? That's just..." My hands balled at my sides with the urge to go back and pummel all of those assholes into dust. Of course, what would probably happen was I'd end up with very sore knuckles and who knew what else.

Loki let out a weary chuckle and stopped. He propped himself against the trunk of a pine and finally met my eyes, a little of their usual mischievous glint coming back. "Well, you see, I made a wager."

"You what?"

He gestured vaguely toward the city we'd left behind. "I saw an excellent opportunity to win the gods a multitude of weapons. Some of the dark elves are quite skilled with their forges, you know. I had one set of brothers fashion Odin's great spear and a ship for Freya's brother Freyr, and then wagered with a different set of craftsmen that they couldn't produce better. And of course they couldn't resist trying. One of the lovely items they produced was Mjolnir."

"I don't really see how bringing the gods a bunch of gifts would have ended up with them attacking you," I said.

Loki's lips curled into a smile. "Well, the wager was for my head, if I lost."

My eyebrows jumped up. "Your *head*?" I was starting to understand all the comments the others had made about the trickster getting into as much trouble as he got out of.

"It had to be something they didn't think they could get anywhere else," he said breezily. "I'd thought the gods would decide in my favor, considering the massive favor I'd done *them*, but, well... The trouble for the dark elves was, I hadn't put my neck on offer, and there was no way for Brokk to take my head without damaging that. So, in the end he settled on the payment you noted." He flicked his fingers toward his mouth.

The story still didn't sit quite right with me. I studied his expression, which was so casual now. "Why wouldn't the gods have decided for you? Why would they have helped the dark elf do that instead of letting you escape if you could? They looked..."

They'd looked almost as if they were *enjoying* carting him off to his doom.

Loki shrugged. "You remember where we are, and what I told you that I'm not, don't you?"

"You aren't exactly a god because you weren't originally from Asgard," I said. "Technically you're a giant. But you're Odin's blood brother. You lived here with the rest of the gods—how long?"

His gaze slid away from me again, with a hint of melancholy he couldn't quite disguise. "It doesn't matter how long. The Aesir have very particular ideas about giants."

"So, they don't like you just because you're not one of them." My mind tripped back to schoolyard taunts, little scuffles in the hallways, with kids who'd made fun of the holes and stains on my clothes, my bluntly chopped hair, before I'd had the wherewithal to at least make myself look as if I fit in. As if that small agony was anything compared to the torment I'd just witnessed. I knew the flavor of it, though. I knew how deep the unfairness of it could sting.

"That's the gist of it," Loki agreed. "The gods and the giants have been at each other's throats rather a lot. I haven't got much love for the people of my birth either, I must admit. For the most part they're a violent boorish lot best left to stew in their own brutality."

"But *you're* not some violent brute," I said. "Anyone with half a brain can see that."

"Why thank you for saying so. But prejudice isn't always so easily dismissed, now is it? And... well, let's just say they have plenty of other reasons to not always feel completely friendly toward me. It's a complicated situation."

That was what Hod had said too. But Hod hadn't made any secret that he blamed a lot of those complications on Loki. I'd never heard Loki criticize any of the gods by name other than teasingly. How much were all those grumblings of Hod's justified, and how much was it simple prejudice?

My jaw set, a quiver of anger running through me. Loki caught my eye and laughed.

"You look so fierce on my behalf. No need to go off avenging me, pixie. It's all a long time in the past now."

Hod had been bickering with him just this morning. Freya had made her comments... My throat tightened.

"Is it?" I asked.

Something new lit in Loki's gaze as he looked back at me, bright but deep behind those amber eyes. He eased himself off the tree. His hand came to my cheek as he bent to kiss me.

It wasn't like the kisses we'd shared before, that instant sear of flames. His mouth moved softly against mine as if we were kindling a fire between us bit by bit, urging it from that first small spark. As if he *needed* my presence, my touch, to bring that flame to life. A swell of yearning filled my chest, and I kissed him back harder.

With a hungry noise, he looped his arm around my waist and tugged me closer. I gripped his neck, my fingers tangling in the silky strands of hair that fell there. Light seemed to flare at the edges of my eyelids.

This must be what it'd be like to stand in the white-hot center of a blaze like the eye of a storm, encased in brilliance and heat but not burned.

The trickster pulled back sooner than I'd have wanted him to, his head staying bowed over mine. My heart thumped out of kilter. "Loki..."

"I know," he said with a flash of a smile, and

straightened up. "No commitments, no proclamations. There are simply moments I can't resist you."

I didn't like the impression I got that he'd just retreated from me. Those words weren't what I'd been going to say. But I had no clue what I *had* wanted to tell him, so I shut my mouth. And opened it again. When I wet my lips, the spicy sweet taste of him lingered on my tongue.

"What do we do now?" I made myself say. "I guess we should look for the others?"

"Or an exit," Loki said. "And there doesn't appear to be one here." His smile turned sharp. "Let's see what else the raven has in store for us in this grand adventure."

8

Loki

"Muninn really did quite an excellent job with this place," I said as we ambled through the forest that bordered our false-Asgard's city. "I suppose it's not surprising, given that she had so many extensive sets of memories to work with. Still, as much as I'd like to smash this construct to the ground and be done with it, I have to give her points for skill."

Ari made a noncommittal sound. She'd drawn in her wings, but the tension showed in her back and shoulders. She was prepared to whip them out the moment she felt we needed to flee. A couple weeks ago she'd held them like they were a burden and now she was relying on them like any other part of her.

She was truly rising to her role as valkyrie. The valkyrie I'd chosen. Even through the whirl of emotions I was trying to smother, I could feel a flash of pride at that.

"So, this really is what Asgard is like?" she said. "Other than little details that have changed since the memories Muninn is using?"

I dragged in a breath of the piney air, warm but with a thread of autumn coolness to it. The raven wasn't worrying too much about keeping her seasons consistent. The rustle of the dried needles under our feet, the slant of the sun between the trees—everything about the illusion rang true. I might have taken this walk a hundred times.

"If I hadn't seen everything I've already seen, I'd believe this *was* Asgard," I said. "When we get to the real thing, you'll find it very familiar. But thankfully with much less sudden emergences of horrifying past events." I winked at her, as if I were joking. As if I couldn't still feel the sting of that leather string around my lips and the sharper jab of all that godly laughter while Brokk had sewn it in.

"And I guess the other gods aren't around very much?" she said. "You said before that you haven't seen a bunch of them in a long time."

I nodded. "The world moved on without us, and some of us took it harder than others. A lot of the lesser gods simply slipped away. Maybe they found some lovely hut on a tropical beach and are living a life of relaxation. Others went off on whatever quests they could make up and never returned. Many of the Vanir returned to their original home—Freyr may still be there. I haven't paid a call in ages. Not that he's likely to celebrate a visit from me."

I gave Ari a grin, but she fixed me with those damned

gray eyes that I was learning didn't miss very much. They shouldn't, with the talents we'd given her when we'd brought her back from the dead in the guise of a valkyrie. But her street-honed instincts clearly took those basic skills to a higher level than the three women we'd sent questing for Odin before her.

Of course, that was why she'd survived and they, as far as we knew, hadn't.

"Well, good riddance to them, if the rest of them were like that." She motioned toward the hall we'd left far behind. A hot prickle of shame ran down my back at the reminder of the scene she'd witnessed before the sewing. Not my most impressive moment, being hauled off by those louts. I'd like to wring Muninn's neck just for dropping Ari there right at that moment.

Our valkyrie hadn't hesitated, though. At least twenty gods around me, and Ari had launched herself at them as if she meant to take them all on in one go, just to free me. It had bothered her that much, seeing the way they were roughing me up, that she'd risked her life trying to stop them.

Literally risked her life, because illusions or not, I'd seen how hard that one punch had hit her. Norns only knew what Muninn might have allowed her creations to do to our valkyrie if she'd kept up the fight. All the fight *I'd* had in me had drained away in that moment, seeing her crumpled on the ground the second before she'd moved again.

A few minutes of embarrassed agony while the damned dark elf stitched my lips was an easy trade for keeping her safe. I'd endured the gods' unruly tempers enough times. She shouldn't have to suffer in my place.

"They had their moments, even the ones I didn't care for much," I said. "I found my ways of getting along with them."

"I guess there must have been something you liked about this place if you stayed here even when they treated you like that, instead of going home."

"Good food, comfortable lodgings, a temperate climate —what's not to love." I shook my head with a bemused smile. She didn't know what she was talking about when she called the realm of the giants my *home*. "You have to remember that my alternative was a rather barren land full of aggressive idiots whose preferred pastime was finding someone's head they could bash in. As you might imagine, I didn't get along with my neighbors there very well either."

"No, I guess not," she muttered, and kicked at a fallen twig. "I just can't... Even *Thor* was ready to hurt you."

She was still stuck on that memory, was she? I supposed it was easier for me to set it aside when I had so many to compete with it.

"None of them meant to do any permanent harm," I said, letting my voice fall into a reassuring tone. "They were simply making sure I fulfilled my wager." Even if it'd been their damned fault I'd lost it in the first place. Odin had done the final judging. "And Thor hadn't known me all that long at that time. Once we'd set out on a few quests of our own, tackled monsters and giant kings and wedding gowns—now that's a story I'll have to share in great detail some time—we developed a much better comradery. You've seen how we are now. No ill-feeling there."

"Hod seems to have some," Ari said quietly.

The twinge of anxiety I'd managed to shove low in my gut jangled through my nerves again. The less we talked about *that* the better. If Muninn hadn't already added it to her schedule of horrors to inflict on us, I'd rather it stayed off.

"And he's welcome to it," I said lightly. "All that glowering keeps him occupied. I expect he'd get very bored if he ever gave it up."

"But—"

"Ari." I stopped and turned to her, setting my hands on her narrow shoulders. A few strands of her dark blond hair drifted across her forehead, and I couldn't resist the impulse to brush them away from her eyes. Perhaps partly because of the heat that sparked in her gaze at my touch. I couldn't imagine ever getting bored of seeing that. Her passion was a gift in all its forms.

"You don't have to worry about me," I said. "I've taken care of myself for longer than you can conceive of. I was happy with the way things were, other than Odin's mysterious absence, and I'm even happier now that you've joined us. The past is just the past, no matter what Muninn tries to make of it."

Ari studied my face as if she were trying to read a deeper truth behind my words. I let only warmth and good humor show in the smile. The rest wasn't hers to carry anyway.

She bobbed up on her toes, pressing a kiss to my lips that I hadn't seen coming. A pleasant shiver passed through my pulse as I leaned in. Oh, yes, I'd chosen well when I'd set my sights on this soul.

I teased my tongue along the seam of her mouth, and her lips parted with an eager sound. Our tongues twined together hotly. She leaned into me, her small curves flush against my chest. I might have taken a few moments in this lull to discover what other sounds I could encourage out of her with the graze of my hands and the flick of my tongue, but just then an irritated yet still elegantly feminine voice traveled through the trees.

"Oh, damn it."

I raised my head, and Ari sank back down on her heels. "I think we may have discovered our missing goddess," I said.

Ari swiveled, hope lighting her face. She was as keen to be done with this place as I was. What memories was she afraid Muninn would conjure? I knew I'd only caught the barest hints of them, she kept them locked up so well.

We hurried through the forest to where it thinned at the edge of Asgard's orchard. In the midst of the gnarled apple trees, Freya was pacing. Her golden hair spilled to shadow her face as she stared at her hands. Her mouth was twisted at a fraught angle.

"Not again," she muttered, and then raised her voice. "Raven, stop this *right now*!"

"I don't think she's likely to listen to you," I said, ambling over. "If anything, she's glad you're distressed." I cocked my head, considering her hands, which looked as smooth and slim as ever. "What exactly is the problem?"

"Don't pretend you can't see it," Freya snapped at

me. "It was your fault the first time. I'm shriveling up all over again. Turning old."

I arched an eyebrow, taking in her perfectly youthful face, and laughed. "No, you're not, oh goddess of beauty. She's playing more memory tricks on you. You're still yourself, as you were when we arrived here. She can't actually change our own forms."

"But..." Freya thrust her hands farther out in front of her as if the distance would give her better perspective. The only line on her lovely face was the furrow down the middle of her brow. Muninn hadn't managed to make her look old, but she had made the goddess look rather ridiculous. I couldn't say I minded this trick all that much.

"He's right," Ari said, pushing past me. She grasped Freya's hands. "I promise you look exactly the same as when I first met you. Don't let the raven mess with your head."

The grip of Ari's fingers against her own must have broken the illusion. The goddess let out a sigh of relief. She patted her face in turn. "What a wretched trick that was."

What a vain woman stood before me. Was that really the *worst* situation she'd ever encountered in her long life? I'd like to see her trade for some of mine.

"So, that was the worst thing you could imagine, dear Freya," I teased. "The most horrifying memory Muninn could pluck from your mind was the time you started to age?"

She grimaced at me. "If I remember correctly, none of

the gods was all that pleased about the situation. No thanks to you."

Ari glanced my way. "How did you make the gods get old?"

I waved my hand. "Another long story. Once upon a time we required the apples of a special tree in this orchard to maintain our youth. Through a total accident, the goddess who picked those apples was kidnapped. With a little quick thinking and quick flying, I retrieved her and all was well."

"I'm not sure how purposely leading her beyond Asgard's walls was an *accident*," Freya said.

"I couldn't have known what the eagle wanted with her," I protested. "Perhaps he was simply looking to have a chat."

Ari swiveled on her heel, taking in the orchard. "Do you still need to eat those apples to stop you from getting old... and dying, I guess?"

"No, thank Asgard," I said. "Our rebirth after Ragnarok removed them as a necessity. As I'm sure Freya has been deeply appreciative of, so that she never needs to worry about so much as a gray hair or a wrinkle."

"Oh, shut up," Freya said. "What's worse—to be upset at losing one's youth or to take glee in seeing it happen to others?"

The retort rankled. I hadn't been gleeful. It was good for the soul to find humor in dire circumstances, not that she'd know much about that. What *had* Odin seen in her to make her his second wife, anyway? Had she addled his brains with beauty and superficial charms?

"I was too busy risking my life fixing the problem to

be taking much glee," I said with a roll of my eyes, keeping my tone light. "I don't recall you contributing much to the effort other than handing over the use of your falcon cloak. I suppose all the rest of your energy was needed to mourn your beauty."

Freya's jaw clenched. "You should have mourned it too, I think. Without that beauty, how would you ever have been able to come up with so many schemes around marrying me off to this creature or that one?"

"Oh, there were plenty of pretty faces around Asgard. I suppose I could have offered up your daughter."

I knew my tongue had flown too fast from the shadow that crossed the goddess's face. Not that her kind had ever shown consideration to *my* children.

She raised her hand to point an accusing finger at me, and the ground shook with thundering footsteps. I spun around to see none other than Thrym himself, once king of the giants, barreling toward us through the trees.

9

Aria

The entire orchard trembled as the massive figure barged toward us. Tall as Loki and nearly as brawny as Thor, the huge man toppled one tree with one swipe of his bulging arm and wrenched another up by its roots with a roar. Swaths of leather hung across his scarred body. A dented iron crown sat haphazardly on his wiry brown hair.

"Oh, perfect," Freya said, backing up to the thicker shelter of the forest. "Now you've brought the king of the giants to life. Just what we needed."

Loki snorted. "*I* brought him to life? I don't recall sending out any invitations."

"You brought up all your schemes, all the ways you used me in your wagers. It seems to me the biggest wager was against him. Where do you think the raven of memory got *this* idea?"

"Ah, I believe you were the one who started venting about my scheming and the various wagers I can assure you I never initiated. Well, at least not the ones involving your hand in marriage, as in-demand as that boon was."

The raging giant tore up another tree and hurled it in our direction. I scrambled backward and ducked behind a pine. "Um, would you two mind settling this argument later and dealing with the giant king who's looking to smash us to pieces now?"

"With pleasure," Loki said, drawing his dagger from his belt with a flash of metallic light. "I have plenty of practice cleaning up the messes the goddess gets into." He beamed at Freya.

"That *I* get into?" Freya sputtered. "If I tried to count the number of times your supposed cleverness put us on the edge of disaster—"

"You don't need to. Continue contemplating your restored beauty and I'll take on the giant."

The giant in question stomped closer. I unfurled my wings, tuning out the rest of their conversation. I, at least, was going to do something to make sure Muninn's latest creation didn't batter us to smithereens. Maybe the hulking giant didn't look all that threatening to the gods, but I sure as hell didn't want to just sit around and wait for him to attempt to crush me.

I flicked out my switchblade and launched myself into the air. The arching branches all around made it hard to get much of an advantage in the air. The giant had almost reached the forest now, a trail of destruction strewn through the orchard behind him. I couldn't match him hand-to-hand, that much was obvious. But if I could find a weak spot like I had with the ceiling in Valhalla... A strike in the right place, and he should crumble into dust like the wargs, like the gods who'd grabbed Loki would have if I'd gotten in a good enough hit.

The eyes, maybe? If I could get close enough to his face to pull that off. The thought of going in there ready to stab that almost human figure in the most vicious of ways made my stomach lurch.

Just a construct out of memories, I reminded myself. Like target practice. Nothing real. No life lost.

Not that I could claim my hands were clean of actual killing after all the dark elves we'd had to slaughter fighting our way to what we'd thought was Odin. That bridge had already been crossed.

Switchblade at the ready, I glided closer to the giant. He snapped a huge branch off one of the apple trees and swung it in front of him like a club. His ruddy eyes focused on me.

"I won't be embarrassed like this!" he snarled. "You'll bring her to me, or you'll all fall."

I had no idea what he was talking about, but he didn't seem interested in bringing me up to speed. Before I'd had a chance to do anything at all, he heaved the branch toward me. I vaulted off a nearby trunk higher into the air, flipping over a tree top. My wings caught me over his head.

The giant slashed upward with the branch faster than I'd expected given his bulk. I shoved myself to the side with a flap of my wings, but the jagged end slammed into my ribs.

I tumbled into another tree with a hiss of pain. My

chest throbbed all across my left side. More bruises to add to my growing collection.

Back in the forest, Loki swore. "Ari!" Freya called out. Splintered wood crackled underfoot as they both charged into the orchard.

I tossed myself out of the way of another swing of the giant's makeshift club, gritting my teeth against the burning in my ribs. My switchblade. My hands were empty. It must have fallen from my grasp when the branch walloped me.

My heart skipped with a sharper panic than even the giant had provoked. That knife was the only thing I had left of Francis. I couldn't lose it here. Muninn's world of illusions might swallow it right up if I didn't get it back quickly.

I scrambled down from the tree I'd landed in. The giant gave another roar. Then Freya leapt between me and that hulking form, her sword gleaming in the sunlight.

"It's me you wanted, isn't it, Thrym?" she said, settling into a fighting stance. "Why don't you come and get me?"

"I demand Freya as my bride!" the giant king bellowed. "A fair trade, the goddess for the god's hammer. I *will* have my price."

She grinned fiercely, her beauty turned blazing. "Here I am. So sad that so many of you forget I'm the goddess of war as much as the goddess of love. And I know exactly which side of me you deserve. Don't you dare lay one more finger on our valkyrie."

The anger in those words sent an ache through my

chest. She wasn't just defending herself but me too. I'd better get on with helping her do it.

I cast around on the ground, searching for my knife. The thud of metal hitting wood rang out behind me. Then a sizzle and a bellow that sounded more pained than furious.

"Oh, and here I thought flames made a lovely addition to your weapon of choice," Loki's flippant voice rang out. "Look at that branch with its merry blaze."

A glint of blue caught my eye. There! I lunged for the switchblade, almost nicking my fingers in my haste to snatch it up. A pang shot through my ribs, but I ignored it. My hand clamped tight around the plastic handle. I spun around to join the battle.

There wasn't much left to join. Freya was slashing at the giant king from one side and Loki taunting him with jabs of his dagger and flashes of fire on the other. One giant, even a king, obviously wasn't much of a match for two powerful gods. And Loki could say whatever he wanted about his heritage, but watching him there, his face glowing with power as he distracted the giant long enough for Freya to whip her blade across the back of the brute's knees, he couldn't have looked more different from the man they were fighting.

That hulking monster was a giant. Loki might have been one once, not that it sounded as if he'd ever really belonged with them, but after all that time among the gods, I couldn't see him as anything but a god himself.

The slice of Freya's sword made the giant topple to his knees with a groan. Freya stepped closer, and at the same moment the hulk snatched a pointed spear of broken wood off the ground and thrust it toward her.

I yelped a warning and hurtled myself forward with my enhanced valkyrie muscles. My outstretched heel smashed into the giant's wrist. His fingers twitched, dropping the spear. Then he was sweeping that hand toward me. I threw myself into the air. He grabbed my ankle, wrenching me backward—and Freya brought her sword to his neck.

"This is as close to me as you're ever going to get," she said, and severed his throat with one swift strike.

No blood streamed down. The giant collapsed completely deflating with a puff of that awful dust.

Freya stood over him, panting. Dirt had streaked her arms and the side of one cheek, but it didn't dull her beauty. I wasn't sure how anyone could forget she was the goddess of war once they'd seen her like that even once.

No wonder Odin had wanted her to be his queen.

"Thanks," I said, coming back to earth with a flap of my wings. I stuffed my switchblade into my pocket. "I didn't know it mattered to you much if I got tossed around."

I'd meant it as a joke, but the words came out a little flat. Freya glanced at me.

"You are *our* valkyrie," she said. "All of ours, even if I didn't have a direct hand in summoning you. If it wasn't for you, we wouldn't be any closer to finding my husband. You've fought for me a lot more than I've fought for you already." The corner of her lips curved up. "And it is nice to have a break from the constant manly posturing. I really didn't want to lose the first chance at proper female companionship I've had in a century or two."

I hadn't really had friends even when I was alive. Too hard to trust anyone that much. No time to devote to them, when it all went to looking after Petey and making more money so I could do the first part even better. It was kind of hard to wrap my head around the idea that a goddess might want my "companionship." I wasn't sure exactly what we were going to talk about once we were done with the basic "explain to me how the hell this or that godly thing works" topics, but I wasn't going to argue with her. Not when she still had that sword in her hand, anyway.

Loki ambled over to join us, swiping the sweat from his high forehead with the sleeve of his tunic. "Well," he said, "we can't say the raven isn't keeping us on our toes. If I ever complained that our lives weren't exciting enough, I apologize tenfold."

Freya raised her eyebrows at him and sheathed her sword. Loki's smile turned sheepish. "Also I apologize for implying you couldn't fight your own battles, dear goddess. Possibly I've underestimated you every now and then."

"Possibly?" Freya said.

"Definitely. I start to think I should have brought the real you with me down to retrieve Thor's hammer rather than Thor in that dress. Although of course then we'd all have been denied the impressive spectacle of the dress, so..."

Freya laughed. "No, I think you made the right

choice there. I wouldn't have missed that sight for anything."

Whatever tension had formed between them before dissolved into the air. I sucked in a breath, and the trees around me wavered.

I froze, studying them. Perking my ears, tasting the breeze, like Hod had suggested. A streak of gray shimmered between two of the trees and disappeared. That ashy taste tickled over my tongue again.

"It's happening again," I said. "The false Asgard is wavering. More than before. Maybe—"

I didn't get the chance to make any suggestions. The ground tipped up, folding the trees down on me, and the smack of a trunk sent me tumbling out of the orchard toward wherever Muninn wanted me next.

10

Aria

Darkness whipped around me. I flung out my arms and released my wings, trying to catch hold of something. A faint sensation tugged at my heart—one of the gods, one of my sort-of creators, someplace nearby. I threw myself toward that impression with all the strength in my body.

I collided with a solid form all lean muscles and smoky scent. *Hod*, I had time to recognize, and then Muninn's constructed world tipped me over again. Both of us fell, sprawling, onto a carpeted floor.

I scrambled off the god, mindful of my knees and elbows. He sat up with a dazed expression, rubbing the back of his head where it'd smacked the floor. "Ari?" he said. His fingers grazed my skin as he found my wrist and clasped it. "Are you okay?"

"Slightly more bashed up than the last time we

talked, but still breathing," I said. The fall had woken up the ache in my ribs. And other smaller aches from earlier today that I didn't really want to count. As glad as I was to see Hod safe and relatively unharmed, I wouldn't mind bumping into Baldur for a little of that healing touch sometime soon. "Where did she send you?"

"Better we don't talk about that," he said grimly.

I'd seen how much the memories Muninn stirred up had affected even unflappable Loki. For now, I wasn't going to push.

I pulled myself into a crouch so I'd be ready to move fast if the situation called for it, but nothing in the room around us looked like a threat. The pale blue carpet was soft under my feet. A twin bed, neatly made with a spaceship-print comforter, stood at our right, a maple dresser and kid-sized chair-and-table set at our left. The window over the table was open, curtain drifting beside it. The breeze carried in the smell of a freshly mown lawn.

"Have you seen any of the others?" Hod asked.

I nodded. "I was on my own at first, and then I ended up with Loki and Freya."

"But no sign of Baldur?"

Oh. Of course he was more worried about his twin brother than anyone else. "No," I said. I wanted to say that I was sure Baldur could withstand whatever Muninn threw at him, but honestly, it was hard to tell what was really going on beneath the light god's bright surface. Sometimes I got the impression he was amping up the shine to deflect anyone from looking underneath.

"She hasn't hit anyone with anything we can't handle

yet," I settled on, and frowned at the room around us. "I don't know what she's up to now. I'm pretty sure we're not in Asgard anymore."

"Not from how it feels to me," Hod said. "I'd imagine this is someplace on Midgard. Do you recognize it?"

I shook my head. "I've never been here before." The only kid's bedrooms I'd ever been in were the ones in my mom's house, and neither mine nor Francis's nor Petey's had ever looked this tidy. The carpet in mine had been so patchy you could practically play checkers on it. There'd been water stains on all of the ceilings from the leaks during bad storms, and a hint of mildew smell that had never quite left because of them. "This is definitely not from *my* memories."

Hod's brow furrowed. His head turned as if he were taking in the room, but I knew he couldn't see it.

"How much can you even tell about where we are?" I asked with honest curiosity.

"From the way the air moves, I can get a sense of the size of the space, where the large objects are. And touch can fill in a lot." He patted the side of the bed. "From the furnishings, I'm assuming bedroom? Not very large. Clean." He paused, his chest expanding with a slow inhale. "Something about it smells familiar. Maybe *I've* been here."

"Do you make a habit of dropping in on random kids?" I said, and tensed as the door eased open. A small figure stopped on the threshold at the sight of us. My heart flipped over.

Oh. Not a random kid at all.

Petey's thin eyebrows drew together as he

contemplated us with his wide gray-blue eyes. Every part of him was exactly as I'd have remembered him, from the mussed golden-blond curls to those skinny legs—legs that poked from beneath shorts starting to fray along the hems. No need to ask whose head Muninn had pulled this part of the illusion from.

Because it had to be an illusion. Petey wasn't really here. But that didn't stop every particle of my body from aching to go to him.

I could go to him, couldn't I? It couldn't hurt the real Petey to give this one a hug, to tell him once more how much I loved him, that I was coming back for him.

Before I'd even finished thinking that thought, I was already moving. Onto my feet, stepping toward my little brother, my arms outstretched. Hod sucked in a breath behind me.

"Ari—"

Oh, God, he wasn't going to be a wet blanket about even this pretend reunion, was he? I ignored him and reached to brush a stray curl from Petey's eyes.

Petey flinched, jerking away from me. He stared up at me with stiffened shoulders. "Who are you?" he said in a quavering voice. "What are you doing in my room?"

The words hit me like a slap across my face. I froze. "It's me, Petey. It's Ari."

He drew back a step. "I don't know you. You're not supposed to be in my room. Mom says no one's allowed to go in there unless they ask me first."

My chest clenched up so tight I could barely breathe. "I just wanted to see you," I said. "You *do* know me. Ari. Your sister. I've been there since you were born."

"You're a stranger. I'm not supposed to talk to strangers."

"Ari." Hod had gotten up behind me. He set his hand on my shoulder, his grip firm but not hard. "This is his bedroom in his foster parents' home. Loki and I came to see it before we dropped him off, that last morning. We should go. She's just trying to hurt you. Don't let her."

"But..." My eyes had gone hot. Petey was still staring at me, his little body rigid. His chin wobbled. As if he was terrified of *me*. "Can't you make him remember? You shadowed the memories over—you must be able to bring them back. It won't count. It's not really him."

"It's not really him," Hod agreed. "And I can't work any magic on him. He's acting the way Muninn wants him to. You let him go once. You can do it again."

I hadn't had to stand there faced with Petey's bewildered gaze before. "Petey, please." I took another step toward him, searching his expression for any hint of recognition. He cringed backward, stumbling right out into the hall.

"Mom!" he cried out in a thin voice. "Mom, help me! There's a stranger—"

A shudder ran through my body. I closed my eyes, set my jaw, and shoved the bedroom door closed.

Footsteps pattered away on the other side. The fake Petey running to his false mother? I threw my shoulders back against the door, my head bowed, my breaths harsh in my throat.

Hod moved toward me, but I held up my hand to stop him. My fingers curled into my palm. I pushed myself off the door, spinning around, glaring into the corners of the room as if I might spot the raven there.

"That was sick, Muninn," I said. "Just *sick*. I don't know why you turned against Odin, but if you think you're somehow the good guy here, you're delusional. You don't just *use* a little kid— Do you have any idea— So Odin seemed a little heartless sometimes? You just proved you're a fucking monster!"

She didn't answer. I hadn't really thought she would. With a strangled sound, I hurled my fist at the wall. It dented the plaster with a satisfying thud and an equally satisfying jab of pain through my knuckles.

"Ari," Hod said, sounding more urgent now.

I leapt away from him, battering the opposite wall with my foot, slamming my heel down on the seat of the chair so the wood cracked. "This is all fake. This is all fake, and garbage, and— I didn't spend years clawing my way out of my mom's house just so you could shut me up in this stupid prison. Let us *out*!"

I took another swing at the wall and then swooped up on my wings and kicked the damned ceiling. Plaster dust sprinkled down. I whirled around, chest heaving, choking on a sob.

Hod stood by the bed, his mouth set in a pained line. Just waiting for me to finish my tantrum. Because what else could anyone call this? What the fuck was I actually accomplishing with all this flailing?

My shoulders sagged. The anger inside me dimmed, but that just left more room for the anguish.

"Are you done, valkyrie?" the god of darkness asked, but his tone was soft, not disapproving.

"I just wanted... I just wanted to hold him one more time."

My voice petered out. I eased forward and leaned my head against Hod's chest. He swallowed audibly. His arms came around me, hugging me to him.

"I know," he said.

"Even if he wasn't real..."

"I know."

I relaxed into his warmth, thinner than Loki's but steadier. He hadn't said much, but just that acknowledgment eased the worst of the pain. Enough that I managed to say, "Well, we're alone now, but I'm not sure there's any way you could kiss this better."

A chuckle broke from Hod's throat. His hands came up to cup my face and gently tilted it back. A hungrier darkness filled his unseeing green eyes. "I could try," he said in a low voice that sent an eager shiver through me.

A different sort of shadow flickered at the edge of my vision. My head snapped around, trying to track it. There. A flutter of wings in the ripple of the curtain.

This time I didn't hesitate. I launched myself away from Hod toward that glimpse of the raven. My snatching hands brushed through a sensation like ruffled feathers—and the room and the god spun away from me.

The world blurred around me. The ground tipped. I tripped over my feet and fell to my knees, which at this point had to be the most bruised part of me.

No carpet this time. Plain wooden boards. A wide-open living room, shelves lined with books along one wall on either side of a stone fireplace. A ceiling fan stirred the humid air overhead. I was surrounded by two empty armchairs and an oversized sofa where two figures sat nestled against each other. A haziness clung to the edges of the space, as if this was more a dream than a physical place. Not that the places I'd been in before here had been real either.

"You could go," the man said. His voice was as thin as his tall frame, his shoulders hunched. His hair fell sleek and white around his slightly pointed ears. A jagged scar cut across the left side of his face. The other side was lined with age. "I know it wasn't easy before. It can't be easy doing it again. I can manage on my own. I doubt Death will let me lose my way."

"No," the woman curled against him said hoarsely. She raised her head from where she'd had her face pressed against his chest, her glossy black hair spilling over her narrow shoulder blades, and I realized it was Muninn. The same loose black dress, the same darkly intent eyes as when I'd first met her.

When was this? *Who* was this? I had the feeling I'd stumbled into one of the raven woman's memories somehow. Had she meant me to? This felt more personal than anything I could imagine she'd have wanted me to see.

"I'm not losing one moment with you," she said, her fingers tangled in the man's shirt. "If I could, I'd conjure more."

He nuzzled her face. "We had plenty. More than I ever had the slightest hope I'd get. You've gotten no shortage of memories out of this, Miss Raven. Don't hold on too hard."

"No such thing," she muttered. Her head bent close

to his again. She pressed a kiss to his lips, and his eyelids slid closed as he kissed her back. My face flushed.

No, I wasn't meant to be watching this at all. But it meant something that I'd managed to tumble from the memories she'd constructed for us into hers, didn't it? There had to be something here I could use.

I'd only started to turn when the scene around me collapsed in on me with a wash of darkness like vast wings battering me. I had just enough time to gulp a breath before Muninn hurled me empty-handed out of her memory.

11

Thor

I couldn't really explain how it happened. The moment anything that felt like a threat came at me, something in my mind and body shifted. The battle fury shunted logic and every other practical consideration to the back of my head. A wave of power rushed through my limbs. With my pulse pounding like a drumbeat in my ears, my feet battered the ground and my hand swung Mjolnir with no thought except how to most quickly connect each killing blow.

Topple them all. Topple them fast. Let the blood flow until not one of them could lay a finger on me and mine.

That was simply my nature. I worked the way I worked, and it had served us well through enough battles across the ages, when we'd had plenty of battles to fight.

The sad thing was, I couldn't say for sure which

battle it was I was re-fighting at this moment. One of Muninn's twists of the landscape had tossed me into a field with a vast array of giants already charging toward me, their teeth bared with war cries and weapons raised. I'd hurled myself forward, hammer at the ready, the second my feet had steadied on the ground.

We'd fought a lot of battles against giants. I couldn't remember any particular one where I'd been on my own, but then, Muninn didn't seem to be aiming for accuracy. Mostly she seemed to be aiming to destroy us.

She could forget about that. I'd bash every one of these giant skulls five times over and still be ready to fight my way back to Ari and the others. One little raven wasn't getting the best of me.

My muscles heaved as I whirled this way and that, slamming the dark-elf-made hammer into a forehead here, a jaw there. Whipping it through a whole line of my enemies, tumbling them like dominos, before it flew back to my hand. If there'd been more of a gap in the fighting, I might have paused to call a clap of thunder and lightning down, but this fray never let up.

The giants might not be taking it easy on me, but this was a cleaner battle than any I'd fought in reality. With each battering, the bodies burst into more dust, until it coated the grass all around. Better than the blood that usually splattered me and my surroundings in the middle of a clash like this. I couldn't say I missed the metallic stink of gore in the air, the flavor of it creeping into my mouth.

But somehow, without the spurts of blood and the

strewn bodies, the roar of the battle fury dulled. I kept fighting, kept bashing the giants that ran at me two or three at a time, because if I hadn't I'd have ended up with a spear in the gut or a club to the head.

I swung left and veered right, trying to summon more of the fervor with the momentum. It didn't work. A weight settled in my gut as I sent the next body flying with a streak of dust.

All these people I'd once killed. All the lives I'd extinguished. They weren't anything more than dust now out there in the real world too. I'd snuffed them out in one thump of my heart, with hardly a thought to any one of them.

The weight in my gut turned queasy. But what could I do but keep fighting until I smashed them all to pieces?

I lashed out to topple a giant who'd rushed up behind me, and realized I was no longer alone.

Ari had dropped down at the edge of the field. She staggered and caught her balance. My gut clenched tighter as she lifted her head to take in the view.

The view of me burying Mjolnir in this giant's head. Slamming it straight into that one's face. More dust rained down, with a faintly sour smell.

I swung faster, harder, my pulse kicking up a notch. The giants might go for her next. They weren't real. If they'd ever been alive, that was a long time ago. I couldn't stop until I'd destroyed them all. Until I'd conquered this damned memory Muninn had thrust me into.

The fiery rage shot back through my veins. A roar rang from my lungs. I hit and kicked and threw in an endless storm of motion as the swarm barreled toward me, sweat trickling down my back. The bodies and shouts blended into a blur. My hammer pummeled flesh and bone until it collided only with empty air.

I swayed to a halt. Were the giants really all gone? Nothing lay around me on the plain except the strewn dust.

My hammer hand dropped to my side. A tremor ran through my muscles. The queasy sensation coiled around my stomach.

Ari was staring. She eased to the edge of the field, clutching her switchblade, her wings unfurled high. The breath she drew in was shaky. Was that *horror* on her face?

"I would have helped," she said. "But I didn't— I couldn't figure out if I might just end up getting in the way. I guess you had it under control."

Her tone turned a bit wry on the last sentence. It prickled at me. Before I could decide how to answer her, another swarm of giants appeared on the horizon. My heart plummeted. Not again. Did the raven really think she could topple me this way?

Ari jerked straighter, her muscles tensing. By Hel, no, I didn't want her in the fray with me, seeing that fury even closer up. Risking the smack of my hammer if my aim didn't fly true, the sear of my lightning.

"Back," I said roughly, waving at her. "Keep away. This is my battle."

Muninn, send her somewhere else. There had to be somewhere better than here. Not that the raven was interested in bettering our situation. If I could fight my way through this scene straight to her, shatter her and her prison... Not that I seemed to have gotten much closer to her so far.

"I can fight," Ari said.

"I don't want you to," I snapped. The giants were almost on me. With gritted teeth, I heaved myself away from her to meet their charge.

It was a smaller group this time. With two stomps of my feet, I sent lightning streaking from the sky into their tightest cluster. I crushed the others even faster than the ones before, my lungs starting to burn with the strain, but the battle fury racing through my brain never quite drowned out my awareness of Ari somewhere behind me. Ari still watching Thor the destroyer.

Often I took pride in that role. But she hadn't seen much else from me in the last two weeks, had she? Teaching her how to pummel her enemies. Burning off frustration by battering the grounds around our Midgard house with my hammer. Destroying all those dark elves who'd swarmed against us.

Or maybe it was simply that having those outside eyes on me was stirring up a twinge of guilt that had always been there but I usually managed to keep buried.

I hesitated a second before I bashed my hammer into the skull of my last attacker. Twisted with rage, that giant's face that didn't look so different than my own probably did. *Brutes*, Loki liked to call them. What would anyone call me?

The body fell with a thump and deflated into a heap of dust. I scanned the field. Nothing else stirred for now.

"Thor?" Ari said. Tentative now. My fingers tightened around Mjolnir's handle.

"How did you end up here?" I asked without turning.

"I don't know," she said. "I seem to be able to kind of reach out toward you all if I come close to you while Muninn is tossing us around. But I haven't figured out how to use that to any real advantage yet. I guess we're always better off together rather than apart. More chances to pick apart her illusions."

Her footsteps rustled across the grass into the drifts of dust. The dust from the bodies I'd toppled, which had felt far too solid as illusions went. My stomach churned. I swiveled around then, pointing in a different direction. "Let's see if we can find a way to toss ourselves out of this place, then."

Ari held still until I reached her and fell into step beside me. I shifted a little to the right to give her more space, but I couldn't help watching her from the corner of my eye.

She flicked her switchblade closed and shoved it in her pocket, her head low. Her wings retracted. In the space of a few seconds, she looked like an ordinary young woman, albeit a determined and sharply pretty one. Even my nausea couldn't stop the current of desire that crept up from low in my belly.

"Are we okay?" she said after a minute, her voice still tentative.

My head snapped around. "What?"

"I just mean... you seem upset. Maybe with me. I don't know. The stuff Muninn's been throwing at us, the tricks she's pulling—I don't know what she could have shown you. I'd like to know we're still all right."

She glanced up at me, worry and confusion shimmering in her eyes. If my stomach had been tight before, it twisted into one massive knot now. She thought I might have some kind of problem with *her*. Shit.

I stopped dead in my tracks, turning to face her. "We're all right," I said. "We're absolutely all right. I'm sorry, Ari. You didn't do anything wrong. This is the first I've seen of you since we got thrown apart in the courtyard. I—I'm glad to see you, just to know you're okay."

She folded her arms over her chest and raised her chin, more of her usual energy coming back. "Then what *are* you upset about? Because something's obviously jerking your chain. Was it something about that battle? Bad memories?"

"Not exactly. I..." I let out a breath in a rush. "I don't want that, the way you saw me out there—the way you've already seen me more times than I'd like—to be the way you think about me. I fight because I need to, and maybe I can find enjoyment in it while I'm in the middle of it, but I don't revel in the killing. I don't seek it out."

Maybe that wasn't entirely true. There had been times, long before Ragnarok, when I'd gone journeying with Loki or one or another of my brothers knowing we'd probably come to blows with someone. But always someone who deserved it. And I hadn't felt that urge to seek out a fight in a long time.

Not since I'd watched my home and all the people in

it consumed in a searing blaze no hammer could defend against.

"Hey." Ari touched my arm. Warmth blossomed under her fingers. "I'm not anyone to judge. How many lives did I whisk away when we took on the dark elves?"

"It isn't the same," I protested. "You don't get lost in it." *You don't wonder whether you really do have control or whether the fury is driving you.*

Her mouth twisted. "I know what it's like to get caught up in emotion. To want to hurt someone so badly you forget everything else in that moment. I don't like it either."

I frowned. My hand moved of its own accord, stroking over her hair. "I'm sure if you've ever felt that way about anyone, they deserved it," I said fiercely.

She closed her eyes, her expression relaxing at my touch. As if she welcomed it every bit as much as I'd wanted to offer it. Skies above, could I be that lucky?

"And the horde you were just tackling didn't deserve it?" she asked.

I wet my lips. "I was defending myself. So, I suppose they did. I don't even remember what we would have been fighting over in whatever memory Muninn pulled them from."

"What's there to feel guilty about then?"

I paused. The answer stuck in my throat. "Sometimes, I regret... We always talked about the giants as our enemy, you know. I didn't even trust Loki for the longest time. But the truth is, my mother was a giantess."

Ari's eyebrows rose as she met my eyes again. "Odin and all his many travels," she said, sounding only amused.

"Basically," I said, a little of my shame at the admission fading. "But he took me back to Asgard as his own, and I always acted as if I were only his. For all I know, I've killed cousins or uncles or who knows what relatives on the battlefield. I never stopped to ask."

"They didn't ask you either," Ari pointed out.

"You don't think there's something twisted about that?"

She shrugged. "I don't think blood means very much. My dad took off before I was old enough to remember him. My mom spent more time cutting me down than taking care of me. I'd sooner help a stranger than her. Being born isn't a promise to anyone."

"But you also wouldn't beat any of them into a bloody pulp."

"I might have been tempted recently," she muttered. She grasped my hand where it was still resting against her hair, curling her fingers around mine. "You want to know how I think about you, Thor? I see strength and devotion and a huge heart that can't stand the thought of anyone under your protection, which is basically all of humankind, getting hurt." She grinned. "Oh, and let's not forget an enormous appetite and the most enthusiastic laugh I've ever heard."

I could almost see my reflection glinting back at me in her gray eyes. I didn't need any of Baldur's special senses to know she was telling the truth. The tension that had been wound through my gut subsided.

Ari's head twitched to the side. Her eyes narrowed.

"What?" I said. Even as the words left my lips, I caught a

hint of something. A dark shimmer, a brief movement, there beyond the stretch of grass and then gone.

"The real world broke through again," Ari said, turning with her hand still clasped around mine. "I saw a little more this time. It was dark, but there was a reddish light, and for a second I felt so hot..." She looked back at me, but her gaze was distant. "It happened when Loki and Freya were talking too."

"I caught a glimpse of something too," I said. "Just now. But only a glimmer."

A smile leapt to Ari's face. "You did? Then the effect is getting stronger. We're getting closer to breaking through. It seems almost like... When it happened before, Loki was apologizing to Freya for not recognizing how great a warrior she is. And just now, I made you think about yourself, about all those battles, a little differently, maybe?" She studied my face.

"You did," I said. "You think that's what caused the break?"

"I don't know. But maybe, when we change our minds about something, or realize we were looking at them the wrong way in the past... That could shake up Muninn's construct, right? Anything that shakes up our memories and the way we think about them should, since she's using those memories as her foundation for this whole place. A little more of that and we'll crack the entire thing apart."

My spirits rose. "We can hope."

"Yeah, we can. Don't let her wear you down, okay?"

She slipped her arms around me, and I bent into her embrace. A smell like clover tickled off her soft hair over a scent like a just-lit flame. Every nerve in my body thrummed with the closeness of her.

When she drew back, her cheek grazed mine. My breath caught. She hesitated there, her lips just inches from mine. Heat rose in the space between us.

"Thor," she said quietly.

"Ari." My voice came out raw. "You and Loki..." The memory of him kissing her in the courtyard jabbed at me.

"...understand very well that I'm not looking to get tied down at the moment," she filled in. Her breath tickled over my jaw. "Which is a good thing, because I don't know if I could be happy just picking one of you. Unless you don't want—"

"To Hel with that," I said, and drew her lips to mine.

She kissed just as sweet as she smelled, the joy of our minor victory rippling between us. I ran my fingers deeper into her hair, and a pleased murmur escaped her. Her body melted into me as if she needed the strength she'd talked about—my strength—to get her through this, if only just in this moment.

The feel of her warm and eager against me almost made me lose my head in a very different way. But it also reminded me that we weren't anywhere near through this prison yet. Reluctantly, I eased back from her. She beamed up at me. The sight of the flush in her cheeks, the rosiness of her lips after that kiss, sent a bolt of lust right to my groin. It took all my self-control not to pull her right back to me.

"Still a lot farther to go," I said.

"Yeah." She turned, her hand on my arm, and her

eyes widened. Her jaw went slack and then snapped shut. "I see—"

I leaned forward to try to make out what she'd deciphered, and an invisible force thrust up between us, ripping Ari away from me. With a shout, I snatched after her. My fingers closed only around empty air.

12

Aria

The world spiraled around me. I tried to shove myself back toward Thor. The wind whipped my body forward, and between the flashes of grass and stone, my gaze caught on a hunched figure behind the thick bars of a cage, a ring of fire licking all around it. The figure raised his head just slightly, showing a silver-flecked beard and one scarred-over eye—*Odin*. A twang ran through my chest: the connection I'd felt when I was searching for him before. That was the real god. But where was he? I had to catch every clue I could...

The smell of ash and something pungently bitter clogged my nose and mouth, and then I was wrenched away from there too. My groping hand closed around solid flesh. I clung on, but the wrist slipped from my grasp.

My ears popped. I fell on my ass on marble tiles that

were so familiar their hard surface was almost a relief. I was back in the Asgard we'd first entered. The massive stone halls loomed around me, hot summer sun streaking between them. In front of me, a huge group of gods—constructs, I had to assume—had gathered in a circle in a smaller courtyard with buildings tight around it. They whooped and hollered at whatever they were watching.

I pushed myself to my feet, catching my balance against the side of the hall I'd landed next to. I hadn't completely lost Thor. He was just straightening up where he must have landed outside the neighboring buildings. His gaze fell on the crowd before it found me. He stiffened, his usually ruddy complexion paling.

What? My head jerked back around to search the crowd, but I was too short to see over the tops of most of the gods' heads. All I knew was that whatever they were doing, it was making them laugh and chatter amongst themselves. It sounded pretty good-humored. But obviously Thor saw something I didn't.

Or remembered something I couldn't have.

I scrambled onto a ledge on the side of the building for a better look. Clinging to the cool stones, I turned toward the crowd again, and froze.

Baldur was standing in a cleared space in the middle of the ring of gods. Distress, a sharper emotion than I'd ever seen from him before, was etched all across his face. One of the gods at the edge of the ring chucked a knife at him, another a stone, another what looked like a carrot. He batted them away with bursts of light from his skin, his mouth twisting tighter.

What the fuck were they doing? Why were they

pelting Baldur, of all people, like that? Hell, they looked *happy* about it, smiles stretching across all those faces, the laughter I'd heard before carrying through the gathering. Like it was a friendly game, all in good sport. Couldn't they see he hated it?

No, they couldn't see anything. They were just constructs. I had to remember that. Constructs Muninn had built and guided like puppets.

But something about this must have come from a memory. It didn't make sense.

I braced myself against the wall to release my wings, but before I could leap off to fly to Baldur, a dark-haired form shoved through the crowd.

"Baldur!" Hod called out.

His twin brother turned. A flash of—was that *panic?* —crossed Baldur's face before his expression settled into one of relief.

Hod hooked his arm around Baldur's and cleared a path with lashes of shadow as he led the light god out of the ring. I watched them go until a flicker in the open space drew my gaze back. My mouth fell open.

Baldur had reappeared in the middle of the ring. But—

My gaze darted back and forth. There were two Baldurs now. The one standing with Hod at the fringes of the crowd, shaking his head with a smile that still looked a bit pained at whatever his brother was saying, and the one who'd appeared out of nowhere in the midst of the other gods.

The new one stood there with arms spread as if

welcoming the projectiles, totally serene. I didn't see any magical glow around him, but when more of the gods took up the "game," tossing a plate, a potato, a spear, every object simply bounced off his body and dropped to the ground.

Huh. This just got weirder and weirder.

Maybe sometime long ago Baldur really had stood there and been pelted, for whatever crazy reason. Someone clearly remembered that.

Thor must have spotted his brothers—half brothers, given what he'd told me about his mother? He was striding around the outer edge of the ring to join them. I hopped down from my ledge and hurried after him. There was only one place I was getting any answers. It was a good sign, wasn't it, that almost all of us had found each other again? We had a better chance of breaking down Muninn's prison the more of our minds we could put together. At least, I hoped so.

"—not going to come to that," Hod was saying in a rough voice when I reached them. "Let's just go. We don't have to put up with her torture."

"I don't think leaving will be enough," Baldur said, his usual melodic lilt eerily subdued. "I can feel it. The things they're throwing at that memory of me. I can feel all of it."

If I'd thought Thor had gone pale before, it was nothing compared to the sallow shade Hod's face turned at that information. His hands clenched.

"Then we'll find the other constructs she's conjured up and stop them before it gets to that point."

"Gets to what point?" I asked, studying their

expressions in turn. "What the hell is going on over there?"

Hod's dark eyes veered toward my voice automatically, and somehow even more color managed to drain from his face. "If we get on with this, you won't ever have to find out, valkyrie," he said, and strode forward, a stick of shadow darting across the ground in front of him. "Has anyone seen Loki yet? One or another of him must be around here somewhere."

"I'll turn him up if he's here," Thor rumbled, and set off in the opposite direction to cover more of the courtyard. Baldur trailed behind his twin. His apprehension quavered so close to the surface that I could sense it where I normally only felt that dreamy calm from him.

I hurried after them, slowing when I caught up with Baldur. "What's the matter? Why were they doing that to you? It really happened, didn't it?"

"It did," he said, his gaze still following his brother. "Hod's right. It'd be better if we simply stop it and don't have to relive the whole event."

"Why?" The other version of him, the remembered one, hadn't looked disturbed at all. He'd seemed to be welcoming the onslaught. "I don't get it. Did everyone just go bonkers one day, or was—"

"Aria." His voice stayed soft, but there was a note of steel in it. "I don't want to go there. Leave it. *Please*."

I'd started to bristle, but the anguish in that last word wrenched at my heart. My mouth snapped shut. "I'm sorry," I said after a moment. "I'll try to help. What exactly are we looking for?"

Baldur glanced down at me then. Some emotion I couldn't read shimmered in his bright blue eyes. He set his hand on my arm and squeezed gently. The touch flooded me with a sudden warmth. For fuck's sake, every one of these gods was way too appealing. I'd just been kissing Thor, and tempting Hod into another kiss before that, and Loki, well... And now one possibly-only-friendly gesture from Baldur had set me alight.

Scratching that itch with Loki the other morning definitely hadn't sated my hunger. I didn't think it'd even taken the edge off. If anything, part of me wanted to find out what it could be like with each of the others even more now. As if this were even close to the time or place for that.

"Loki should be around here somewhere," Baldur said. "Possibly two of him as you can see two of me. And there may be another Hod. The more of them we can spot, the better."

"On it." I gave him a little salute and pushed myself off the ground with a flap of my wings. They did come in handy at times like this.

Someone in the crowd chucked an axe at the memory-Baldur. It glanced off his skin, and the gods all cheered. I grimaced at them, not that they seemed to be able to see me, and soared over the ring.

Freya's bright head came into view. She hustled over to Hod where he was circling the crowd. Her expression was already tensed. They all knew what was happening here, or about to happen. All of them except me. Whatever it was, it was clearly going to be awful.

I wheeled, and a shock of pale red hair gleamed

between the shadows of the buildings. Loki sauntered out of a side path at the other side of the courtyard. He took in the scene, and his lips pressed flat.

When even he couldn't find anything amusing in a situation, you knew it was really bad.

"Hod!" I called with a gesture toward the trickster, and then remembered the blind god wouldn't be able to see my pointing arm. But Thor had heard me too. He hustled around the crowd to join Loki, and the two of them hurried to where the other three had stopped. I dove down, my feet touching the ground just as all five of the gods met up.

"You haven't found the spot yet?" Loki was saying.

Hod had bristled. "After all this time, with all the activity, it's hard to mark it exactly."

"Well, come on then. Obviously I have to do everything around here."

Loki stalked off around the ring, and the rest of us hurried after him. His gaze twitched from side to side. Then his shoulders tensed, and he sped up to a lope.

I saw why a second later. The sun caught on another head of pale red hair, this one partway through the crowd. The second Loki. I propelled myself off the ground with my wings for a better view.

Not just a second Loki. Another Hod, as youthful as always but with hair falling a little longer around his face, stood next to him. The memory-Loki was guiding him forward with a hand on his elbow. The memory-Hod was clutching a small branch, a few leaves as dark green as his eyes still clinging to it. The tip had been carved to a point.

The real Loki cursed and shoved his way into the crowd, but the other him and the other Hod had just reached the inner edge of the ring. That Loki bent close to Hod's ear as if to murmur something to him. He drew back the other god's hand, the one that held the branch, and gave a brisk nod.

My Loki lunged forward, grabbing the other Loki by the arm. The other Hod had already flung the branch forward. It spun through the air. The memory-Baldur turned to face his brother, and the branch struck him right over the heart.

Struck him and stabbed into his chest, blood welling up all around it.

A choked sound broke from my throat. I dove down, but Baldur's legs were already sagging. The god of light collapsed on the ground. Blood pulsed from the wound to pool on the marble tiles. Slowing as his heart stopped.

I hit the ground so hard I fell to my knees. They smacked the hard stone, but I hardly felt the impact. Baldur's head lolled. His bright blue eyes were glazed. My stomach heaved.

The crowd around us had gone quiet. A wail cut through the stunned silence. More and more voices joined it, with gasps and sobs, in a vast chorus of mourning.

I'd only dragged in one ragged breath, and the wails cut off as quickly as they'd risen up. I lifted my head. The crowd had disappeared. There was no one left but the real gods and the Baldur from their memories, lying there in that pool of his blood. Looking very, very dead.

He couldn't really have— I dropped my face into my

hands, my heart thudding painfully hard. That sense I'd had that he was hiding something. The conversations about burying unpleasant memories so deep you never had to face them. That comment he'd made, with such a strange note in his voice it'd stuck with me: *I wasn't there for Ragnarok.*

Because he'd died before it ever happened.

Died... because Hod had thrown some special branch at him. Because Loki had guided the god of darkness there.

My gaze jerked up. The real Loki, my Loki, was standing in the courtyard where he'd tried to stop his old self. A shadow had dulled his normally brilliant eyes. His jaw worked.

A thump at the edge of the courtyard drew both our attentions. The real Baldur had turned away, his hand braced against the front of one of the halls as if holding his body up. His shoulders shook and tensed and shook again.

I can feel it, he'd said just a few minutes ago. *I can feel all of it.* What was he feeling now? Was he dying like his counterpart? I pushed myself off the ground.

Hod spun toward Loki, his face even harder than usual.

Loki spread his hands. "I tried," he said. "I tried to stop it."

"Not that there would have been anything to stop if you hadn't done it in the first place," the dark god spat out.

My legs wobbled. "Would someone please tell me what the hell just happened?" I said. "Is Baldur okay?

Why was *anyone* throwing anything at him? How could that little branch..."

"I'll be—I'll be all right," Baldur forced out, but his voice was weak and ragged. Hod glanced toward him, shifting and then tensing as if he wanted to go to his twin but didn't at the same time.

Thor stepped toward me. He set a steadying hand on my back. "A long time ago—not that long before Ragnarok—Baldur and his mother, the goddess Frigg, started having dreams about him dying. Frigg was so worried for him she went around the realms asking every object to vow it would never hurt him. But she passed over the mistletoe. She said it seemed too young and meek to hurt anyone."

The initial scene made a little more sense, knowing that. "So everyone figured they'd test out those vows?" I said. From what I'd seen, it'd worked. Nothing had hurt Baldur in the slightest.

"Like a game," Loki said in an edged voice. "A stupid, careless game. Let's pretend to kill the god so recently terrified of dying."

"Better than actually killing him," Freya said.

"I didn't, did I?" the trickster said, whirling around. "I brought the mistletoe. I offered it to Hod. It seems to me he willingly took it. He wanted to join in, and I let him."

"You knew it might really hurt him," Hod snapped back. "Who sharpened its end into a spear? You didn't tell me what I was holding."

"You didn't ask. Did you even really want to know?"

An angry flush swept across Hod's pale face. "You can't be suggesting I was hoping for that outcome."

"How should I know?" Loki demanded. "The bitterness was wafting off you like the stink of a skunk. It was a stupid game played by stupid gods trying not to see the world was on the verge of collapsing, and I gave you the means to open their eyes."

"You killed him," Hod said. "You killed him with my hand, and for that they killed me too, and you went off merrily free. And we all know how you repaid the rest of Asgard."

Loki waved a hand at him. "Look at you even now. What matters to you more: having a go at me, or looking after your beloved brother?"

"You..." The word came out strangled. Hod threw himself at the trickster.

"Stop!" I cried out. Thor caught his brother by the shoulder. He glowered at Loki.

Loki looked from the two of them to the shaking Baldur and then to Freya, who was watching the scene with accusing eyes. He turned to me. There was a wildness in his movements, in his face, that I'd never seen before, desperate and vicious. I took a step back.

"It really happened like that, didn't it?" I said. "You really killed him." Not a trick. Not a little trouble he could talk his way back out of. Cold, deliberate murder. And he was defending it even now.

My stomach lurched again. Loki's expression shuttered.

"Fine," he said. "This is the way it always is, the way it always was. As if you had the slightest idea... Enjoy your high horses in your glass houses."

He spun on his heel and swept away on his shoes of

flight. Hod looked as if he might try to chase him, but he moved instead to his twin. Freya caught Thor's gaze and shook her head as if to say, *What a shame, but what else could we expect?*

My gut was still knotted. I swayed back another step, and found myself flipping backward out of the courtyard, into the darkness of Muninn's mind.

13

Aria

I stumbled straight into a room I guessed was a study. A big oak desk stood at one end, surrounded by bookshelves. At the other, where I was now standing, two old-fashioned maroon armchairs faced each other with a little bow-legged table between them. My sneakers sank into the rich pile of the rug beneath them. A slight smoky smell hung in the air, but this time it was wood smoke, not the chemical ash I'd noticed before. From the fireplace in the corner, I guessed.

Whose memory was this? The furniture looked human-made, not the grand scale I'd seen on Asgard, but it was smaller and cozier than the study in the gods' Midgard home that seemed to be mostly Hod's domain. I'd never been in a house other than that one that even had a study.

I turned to try the door and found the wall where

there should be one was solid, nothing but yellow-gold rose-print wallpaper. A claustrophobic itch crawled across my shoulders despite the room's cozy warmth.

A black shape fluttered past me. I jerked around to see a raven land on the top of one of the arm chairs. It cocked its head at me in a much too familiar gesture. Then, with a twitch of its body, the bird transformed into a woman.

Muninn settled into the seat of the chair, the skirt of her loose black dress tucked under her slim palm legs, her dark eyes watching me as intently as when she'd been in raven form. My pulse hiccupped. This whole time, she'd been hiding away from us, casting me off again every time I caught a glimpse—or bringing buildings down on me. What did it mean that she was revealing herself now?

"Valkyrie," she said in her sweetly hoarse voice. "Why don't you sit down?"

"Well, for starters, after everything you've thrown at me so far, I feel safer on my feet," I said.

She blinked at me as if she didn't totally understand what I was referring to. She might have looked like a person right now, and she was definitely as smart and aware as any human being I'd met, but from what I'd seen of her so far, her mind was as much raven as it was human. I wasn't sure how much concepts like fair play or compassion applied where she was concerned.

"I promise no harm will come to you in this room," she said. "And that I will not send you out of it until we're finished speaking."

The words rang with a magical force that sent an

eerie tingling over my skin. I'd spent enough time in the company of gods to believe she was bound to that vow.

As much as all the things Baldur's mother had begged had been bound to their vow? My stomach clenched all over again, remembering the scene she'd torn me out of. But my body was still mottled with aches and pains, my legs a little wobbly. Sitting, if I had that promise, might not be such a bad thing.

I sank into the other chair, my gaze never leaving the raven woman. She flicked her sleek black hair back from her face with a fluttery gesture and considered me in return.

"Would you like something to eat?" she asked.

Despite all the tension in me and the horror of what I'd just witnessed, a pang shot through me. I licked my lips. "Something I *can* actually eat?"

"Of course. I'm not that horrible a host." She motioned to the table, and a silver plate appeared. It held a dinner roll stuffed with cheese and sliced meat, a bunch of grapes, and a raspberry tart.

Saliva sprang into my mouth as the bready scent reached my nose. I managed not to snatch up the sandwich but to grasp it firmly and raise it calmly to my mouth. I braced myself as I bit down—and my teeth sank into real bread, real cheddar, real ham.

In a matter of minutes, I'd gulped the whole thing down, the grapes and the tart too. Who knew when Muninn might decide to take them away? I couldn't help licking the last crumbs from my fingers, since I couldn't count on her being this generous again. Somewhere in there a glass of water had appeared on the table too. I grabbed in and drained it.

Muninn sat quietly, watching me, through the meal. When I finished, wiping my mouth with the back of my hand, she gave me a small smile.

"Refreshed?" she said.

"Yes." I hesitated. "Why did you give me that? Why am I here?"

She shrugged. "I simply wanted to talk. You've seen a lot since you arrived here. What the gods of Asgard are capable of. How they make their fun. How they settle their grievances. Not quite as pretty a picture as I'd guess they painted you of the place, is it?"

"They hadn't told me all that much about it," I said honestly. Had she tossed us into those memories for that reason too? Not just to torment each of us with glimpses of the past, theoretical or actual, but to put on some sort of demonstration? Just like she'd tried to paint Valhalla in the negative light of her memories. My hands clenched in my lap.

"I can't imagine you're very impressed either way," she said. "And there's so much more I could show you. Ages and ages of petty in-fighting and prejudice, callousness and violence. That's what the gods are made of, it seems."

"All of that was a long time ago," I said. "They haven't acted anything like that in the time I've been with them."

"Other than just now, when I *made* them remember their past?" Muninn leaned forward. "They've put on a little show for you. For their precious valkyrie and her precious mission to find Odin. They don't give a damn about you, any more than Loki gave a damn about Baldur's life, any more than Thor gave a damn about the endless lives he slaughtered, any more than Odin gave a damn whether his warriors were really all that worthy."

"Is that why you're putting us through all this? Because you don't like things they've done? It's kind of the pot calling the kettle black to accuse *them* of being cruel. How many times could any of us have been killed by the stuff you created in there?"

The raven woman didn't look fazed by my accusation. "If you had just sat tight, accepted the realm I'd given you, I wouldn't have needed to do anything at all. But you were trying to break out. Measures require countermeasures."

I had the feeling I wasn't going to convince her of my point of view any time soon. "Okay," I said. "Fine. That still doesn't answer why I'm here." Or why she'd shut us in this prison in the first place, not that I expected her to tell me about that.

Her smile came back. "I'm hoping you'll see reason," she said. "You've made your feelings about the holding cell I've created very clear. And it's true, I have no real dispute with you. You simply happened to be in poor company. So I wanted to make you an offer."

My body stiffened against the chair's soft padding. "What kind of offer?" I pressed when she paused.

"Leave them," she said, her eyes intent on me. "Let them deal with their memories alone. They suffer nothing but what they brought on themselves anyway. What I do isn't easy on my own. I could use a valkyrie on my side. They don't deserve your loyalty."

I caught a laugh. "And *you* do?"

"I would earn it. I don't expect something for nothing as they so often do. You'd have your freedom too. You wouldn't serve me—we'd be allies. Equals."

"Do you really think after all the times you lied to us, all the danger you've put us in, that I could ever trust you?"

She blinked, more slowly this time. "I can admit that you shouldn't have taken their punishment with them. You can escape it now. If you choose to return to them... I do what I have to in order to keep the holding cell stable. I can't promise anything about what you might see from your own mind."

My thoughts tripped back to Petey in his new home. A shiver ran down my spine. "If you use my brother again—"

Her eyebrows lifted. "Which one? There are so many things I've seen in your memories that you might want to avoid."

I swallowed hard. This was an offer, sure. It was also a threat. Just thinking about all the things from my past she might decide to dredge up if I refused chilled me down to the bone.

I didn't have to find out what else she'd put me through. I could accept her offer. Leave the gods and goddess behind. See what awaited me outside this room that I had to assume wasn't Muninn's real surroundings either. Maybe I'd have better opportunities to get the others free from the outside.

Or was I just thinking that to justify sparing myself?

I shifted in the chair, resisting the urge to draw my knees up in front of me like a child. "How would it work? This alliance? How could I know I could trust you to keep your word?" *How are you planning on making sure I keep mine?*

Muninn spread her dainty hands. "A simple vow should cover all concerns. On both sides. We'll both want some security in the deal, I assume." Her eyes glinted as if she'd read my thoughts as well as my memories.

If I took a vow of loyalty, I'd be stuck with her. And it would probably stop me from doing anything to help the gods she was against. I sucked in my lower lip.

Every part of me balked at the idea of wading back into those memories—both mine and those of the gods. I didn't know what to think of Loki or Hod after the scene I'd witnessed. What other secrets did Thor and Freya and even Baldur have that I might not have realized yet? They'd all hidden a lot from me, hadn't they?

But even as my anxiety gnawed at me to cut myself loose, other sorts of memories surfaced. Hod sitting with me on the roof across from Petey's foster family's house as I said my good-byes, offering words to steady me, taking me in his arms when I'd reached out to him. Baldur healing the many wounds I'd taken with his normally unshakeable smile. Freya talking through my discomfort with me, sharing her own frustration that she couldn't do more for her husband. Thor lending me his hammer so I could burn off some of my tension, kissing me just now with such unexpected vulnerability.

And Loki. My trickster. My stomach knotted all over again remembering the way he'd talked to Hod, the way he'd defended how he'd guided Baldur's death. How could that be the same man who'd brushed aside the way the gods had tormented him before, who'd reassured me that *I* didn't need to be angry on his behalf?

I'd known he might be dangerous. Was that his nature, like the fire he could conjure? Simmering hot below the surface until a sharp gust sent him flaring, burning everyone around him?

I didn't have all the answers yet. I'd barely had a chance to ask the questions. Muninn had suggested that the gods had expected a lot from me without giving anything in return, but they'd given me a lot. I wouldn't be alive at all if not for them. I wouldn't have these powers. They'd been there with me, supporting me, every step of this journey until now.

No. I couldn't abandon them. Hell, even the thought of what they might be going through right now made my heart ache.

"Thanks for the offer," I said, standing up, "but I'm going to have to say no thanks. So, go ahead and do whatever you've got to do. I'm with them."

Muninn's gaze followed me as she stayed put in her chair. Her jaw tightened. "Have you really thought this through?"

What did it matter to her that much anyway? In there, I was just one more person for her to torment, wasn't I? I couldn't see how she'd need a helper that much, one she couldn't just find somewhere else among the dark elves or whoever.

I paused. It wasn't really about how I could help her

out here, was it? It was about how I might hurt her in there.

"You're right," I said. "I hadn't thought it all the way through. You don't even really want an alliance with me, do you? You're just worried about me being in your little 'holding cell' because I don't share that many memories with the others. It's too easy for me to see through your constructs when I'm with them. Too easy for me to shake up their memories with an outside perspective."

"You don't know anything," she said, her tone turning haughty. Her chin rose.

"I know I'm going to shatter this prison," I shot back. "I know you know it too, or you wouldn't be scared enough of me to try to wine and dine me. Maybe I should be the one making you offers. Let us out now, and we won't—"

She made a strangled sound and thrust out her hands. "Have the world you want then. It'll only get worse."

I stumbled backward—and out through an open door that hadn't been there an instant before.

14

Baldur

I tried to hold on. With every shred of strength I had in me, I tried. But the darkness swelled from right inside me, blotting out the courtyard and the wall I'd been braced against and my fellow gods. Blotting out *me*. I was nothing more than a thought in an infinite void, a dark cold expanse that went on and on and yet closed around me so tightly I struggled to breathe.

Silence echoed in my ears. No taste met my tongue, no scent reached my nose. No sensation touched me at all except frigid nothingness.

My mind shuddered. I had the impulse to close the eyes I could no longer feel, as if I could shut out the darkness with more darkness. Maybe they were already closed. I tried to grope and flail, but I couldn't tell if I was even moving. A shudder rattled through my thoughts.

Not this again. By all that was sacred, *no*.

It would be over. I grasped on to that fact the moment it rose up in my mind. This wasn't forever. It was only a trick of Muninn's. She was emulating the cold dark of death I'd lingered in for years and years that seemed like an eternity, when I'd thought it might be an eternity after all. I'd had no idea, that first time, that I'd be reborn. For all I'd known, I was destined to drift in that chilling nothingness until my thoughts completely disintegrated and—

No. It wasn't doing me any good remembering that fear. I had to fight this. Muninn wanted to destroy us, and I couldn't let her.

If only she hadn't chosen her weapon so well.

Focus on what came after. Focus on the warmth and the light. Light to burn away the darkness she'd summoned. I tightened my hold on my thoughts and turned them in that direction.

It *had* been warm and light, that moment when I'd opened my eyes to a field on the edge of Asgard, tall grass hissing around me in a late spring breeze, the sun beaming overhead. With all that sensation around me all at once after so long in the void, I hadn't known how to process it. I just lay there for what felt like hours, soaking it in, my thoughts settling behind a fog of calm I summoned with the light. I needed that fog to drown out everything before: the cold and the dark and the nothingness.

Maybe it hadn't been all that long, though. When I'd stood up in the field, other gods and goddesses all around me were just finding their feet too. We turned, taking in each other and the halls of our great city, tall and shining, beyond the grass. A few of the others had started to laugh in pure delight. Tears streamed down one goddess's face past her brilliant smile. I'd smiled back automatically. I didn't know what they'd been through, but I could understand their joy.

I'd turned again and found myself face to face with Hod.

The last time I'd faced him—*no*. I cut off that thought, that memory, and the flare of darkness that clung onto it.

"Brother," he'd said roughly.

I couldn't say how he'd recognized me. We'd been by each other's side so often from the moment we were born, he probably could have read my presence in the rhythm of my breath, in the shift of my weight against the ground. He'd told me once that he could feel the light in me even if he couldn't see it.

I opened my arms, and he stepped into them. We'd never hugged all that much even as children, but that moment had seemed like the time for it. He'd squeezed me hard and stepped back, tension still strung all through his body.

"Brother, I—"

I cut him off instinctively, my mind sinking deeper into that fog of light. "It's good to be back, isn't it?" I teased my fingertips over the blades of grass. "It's wonderful."

He swallowed with a bob of his throat. "Yes. Yes, it is. Everything feels as it was. Does it look the same?"

I considered the city again. Was the gleam slightly

more muted? I didn't know if I could trust my memories from before the void. It had crept through every part of me. Tarnished every image I'd ever held.

A cold shiver ran through me. I sank deep into the haze.

"As magnificent as it ever was." I beckoned him with a brush of my fingers against his sleeve. "Let's go home."

We hadn't made it all the way to the city in that first go. We'd only taken a few steps when a tall imposing figure moved to join us.

Our father, the Allfather, had been reborn with his travel-worn cloak draped across his shoulders and his dented broad-brimmed hat still shading his single bright eye and the scar of the other. He looked as if he hadn't so much come back from the dead as from a ramble around Midgard.

"My sons," he'd said in his low voice. He clapped Hod on the shoulder and pulled me into a brief but tight embrace. "It's been too long."

His gaze traveled across the field and paused on Frigg, our mother. She was watching us from where she'd hesitated in the middle of the crowd of reborn Aesir. Something in Odin's face darkened.

I didn't understand it then, didn't let myself focus on it long enough to ask, but later I learned their marriage had started to splinter not long after my death. He'd blamed her for the vows, for the game that had followed them and its tragic end. More, it'd seemed, than he blamed Loki, which had never made a lot of sense to me in the fleeting moments I'd let myself consider it. But my father's deeper thoughts were often mysterious.

He prodded my side then, firmly but not hard enough to hurt. "The vows that were made on your mother's behalf won't apply to you in your rebirth," he said, his tone going a bit gruff. "Don't tempt fate by pretending invulnerability."

"Of course not," I said.

I'd seen my own wife then: the lovely Nanna. She darted through the grass to join us and linked her arm around mine, tipping her head against my shoulder with a sigh that was almost a sob. Even as I raised my hand that first time to draw her closer to me, the fog I'd wrapped around myself crept into the space between us.

No matter how much light I summoned to cloud out the past, I knew I wasn't the god she'd married. I'd left too much behind in the darkness of the void. Not many marriages of Asgard had survived the first century after Ragnarok, but ours had crumbled faster than most.

In the present, in Muninn's false-void, I shivered. There wasn't much warmth in the memory of our falling apart. If I stayed there, the raven won. I cast my mind further forward instead.

The only figure of real importance I hadn't seen in the field that day was Loki himself. It was only some time later he'd come to me as I'd taken a stroll through the orchard. Another bright spring day, but I couldn't say whether it'd been just a few weeks after our reawakening or the next year. The days had blurred together with the haze around my thoughts.

"Oh, Light One," he'd said in his jaunty tone, falling into step beside me. But he'd kept a cautious distance between us, his head dipping somewhat deferentially. "I hope there aren't any hard feelings—bygones left to be bygones and all that? I've never borne *you* any animosity. The circumstances being what they were—making the best of a bad situation..."

"I hold no grudges," I told him. I didn't want to feel anything, didn't want to think anything about the time before the field at all.

He'd given me his brightest grin, brilliant enough to rival a blazing fire, and we'd never spoken of it again. You could say a lot of things about the trickster, but one thing he knew how to be without flaw was circumspect, if he felt he owed you that much.

That memory sent me sliding back into the dark of the present. The sharp words thrown back and forth between my brother and Loki as I'd spiraled into this place. I tried to squeeze those images out of my mind.

The cold squeezed tighter around me at the same time. Darkness choked the throat I couldn't otherwise feel. A jolt of panic scattered my thoughts.

Light. I needed light. That was the only way I could fight this.

Normally I could will a warm glow out of myself simply by wanting to. Light clung to me and wound through me the way shadows came to Hod. I willed a burst of brightness into the space around me, as if I didn't already know how that would end.

The light and the warmth vanished into the void, swallowed up the second they left me as if they'd never been there. The chill seeped even deeper.

I propelled more light out and felt it leached away from me before I caught control of myself. There was no point in feeding brightness to the dark. I had to pull back inside myself, hold on to the light I could find there. Just staying sane would be a victory. Muninn could wound me, but only as deeply as I let her.

There'd been so much light in my life, even in the years waiting for Odin's return on Midgard. Loki, eyes always gleaming with mischief, hair shining like fire, beaming as he made his sly jokes. Thor's jovial voice as he roared with laughter and passed on a plate of food while we sat by the crackling hearth. The walks I'd taken with Freya through the countryside, both of us quiet in a mutual understanding that we wanted company, not conversation.

And Hod, who dwelled in his own darkness so much that even a glimpse of light from him could fill a room. The times he'd stopped by the music room and leaned back to listen to me play, a rare smile crossing his face... I treasured every memory like that.

I'd seen his smile more in the last couple weeks, when he watched Aria. Our valkyrie lit something in my brother without even realizing it. But then, she had almost as much fire in her as Loki did. My memories of her glinted in my mind: her lilting voice as she'd sung along with my guitar, her grin warm or fierce depending on the situation in front of us.

Maybe not fire. Her strength and brightness were like she was made of steel forged out of sunlight.

Even as I thought that, the memory I'd been hiding myself in dimmed. A wash of cold crept through it, dulling Ari's shine. I whipped my thoughts from her to

Hod, to Loki, to our other companions, but the darkness chased after me.

That had happened before too. The void had crept inside me until it'd filled every crevice in my head, tainted even my fondest memories.

I couldn't let that happen. I couldn't fall into that endless pit again. I'd left too much behind the first time. What would be left of me if I lost myself a second time? The others, all of them—they needed me in this battle.

The panic shivered through me. I tried to twist and pin down my thoughts, but they flitted every which way, fleeing the fingers of cold. I hadn't been ready for this.

I hadn't let myself be, I'd been so afraid to even consider it might happen.

A different memory rose up, one not bright or warm but tinged with regret. Hod had come to me wanting to talk about that moment in the courtyard, about what I might have gone through afterward, just a few days ago. I'd turned him away. I'd told him there was no need. I'd snapped at him to stop.

I'd been wrong. How had I ever convinced myself that I'd somehow made my peace with the past? I simply hadn't dwelled in it and had called that peace enough. But now that I was forced to dwell in it again, I didn't have the slightest idea how to fend it off. I had nothing but the panic and the dread rising up beneath it.

Just breathe. I clung onto that idea as closely as I could. Just breathe with the lungs I couldn't feel, the air I couldn't taste. In and out. Think of nothing but that. I *had* to hold on as long as I could. Eventually this would be over. Eventually Muninn would decide I'd had enough. Maybe I couldn't fight, but I could endure.

Let me not have lost too much by the time she gave in. And if I ever got another chance to talk, to push aside the haze and tackle the truth with someone who cared—skies above, let me not waste it.

15

Aria

I should have known I'd end up somewhere bad after
Muninn's warning, after the anger on her face. But
somehow I wasn't prepared to find myself skidding to a
stop in the living room of my old house, with the sour
smell seeping from the stained carpet and the sofa
cushions sagging in the dim light that made it past the
blinds. Every muscle in my body tensed instinctively,
even though I was alone in the room.

Alone for that brief moment. I spun around, and
Mom appeared in the doorway to the kitchen, her
expression taut as a wrung towel.

She jabbed a finger at me. "Don't give me that look.
As if you deserve half the time and energy I already give
to you. Why don't you stay in your room where I don't
have to see that pinched face of yours? You don't like
dinner? Get a job and buy it yourself."

It was a patchwork of rants from across my childhood. Lord only knew which dinner I'd complained about—a lot of the time she'd just tossed a few pieces of bread and some margarine on the table and told Francis and me to go at it. By the time I was thirteen, a year after his death, I *had* started picking up odd jobs to keep me out of the house and put a little more food in my belly. She'd been making that suggestion since I was something like five, if she bothered to answer a complaint at all instead of just rolling her eyes and turning her back on me.

"Why don't *you* get a job?" I snapped back now before I had a chance to think better of engaging. My nerves jittered. Who else was going to appear? That haircut—lank, shoulder-length, and bleached a yellower blonde—that was circa the Trevor years. An icier shudder ran through me.

"Don't you talk to me like that, you little bitch!" Mom screeched. I was already diving for the door at the other end of the room. I dashed through the mudroom that was more of a trash bin, out to the backyard where the rusted swing set left by the house's former owners was creaking.

If I got far enough away, would Muninn just throw me back here? Might as well find out. I'd rather be running than waiting around for the real horror show to start. What I really needed was to find at least one of the other gods. The raven woman had all but confirmed it with her reactions. When we were together, challenging the memories, her prison got so much shakier.

I scrambled over the dented chain-link fence and dashed down the neighbor's driveway. The growl of a familiar engine, the one that had taught me to burrow myself deep under my covers if I heard it arriving late at night—as if that would protect me any—carried down the street.

My heart stuttered. I threw myself in the opposite direction.

I was stronger than that now. If he came at me, if Muninn forced the issue, I'd slit his fucking throat. The thought was sickening and satisfying at the same time.

I rounded the corner, past the laundromat and off-brand burger place. How far was she going to let me run? Maybe I'd just make for the park. Have a nice little jog to stretch my legs while I figured my way out of this.

I veered toward the next street, and Loki came stumbling out of an alley to my left. He managed to right himself with such assured grace you'd almost have thought he tossed himself around like that on purpose.

His bright gaze snagged on mine. "There you are. Do you have any idea how difficult it is to track you through this memory maze?"

I slowed as I turned to face him, but I took one step back and another. A different sort of tension had wound around my gut. While I'd wanted to find one of the gods, I wasn't sure I was ready to face this one. Loki looked a lot calmer than the last time I'd seen him, but the image of his vicious expression, the cutting edge to his words, lingered way too clearly. How could we fight together if I couldn't trust him not to stab me in the back?

"From what I remember, you were the one who ran off on us," I said.

He grimaced. "Somehow I doubt I'd have made the

situation any better if I'd stayed. I thought I was ready, even if she dredged that up, but... Ari, it wasn't the way it looked."

"You didn't set up Hod to murder his own brother?"

"I—" He cut himself off with a rough sigh. "It's complicated. I'm just asking you not to judge from that one moment when the entire picture is so much larger."

"Complicated," I repeated. "I can't really think of any complications that would make doing that okay. You know, Hod said the same thing, and I was starting to think he was just excusing away hating you for no good reason. But seeing that, I'm surprised he can even stand to be around you."

Loki winced. He held out his hand to me. "Pixie..."

The cajoling note in his voice wrenched at me, too hard. I wasn't here for him to sweet talk me into sympathy. I didn't trust myself not to be swayed when I shouldn't be. He was too damned slick.

"Don't," I said. "Don't call me nicknames, don't act like I'm on your side here. If you want to help find a way to break this place down, great. Let's stick to that. I want to get out of here, not talk about ways to justify murder."

I spun around. Loki hurried after me.

And the vision of my childhood neighborhood split apart with a thunderclap.

I spun faster, my ears ringing, as darkness closed in around me. My pulse thumped. I waited for the dark to spill me out into some new memory... but it didn't.

My sense of my body stilled, and then started to fade. I was floating there in the black and the cold. What the fuck kind of torture was this?

I flipped around, as much as I still could move with my skin and the muscles beneath it going numb. A thread of sensation ran through my chest. One of my gods, one of the other gods who'd helped form me as a valkyrie, was somewhere close. Not Loki this time, I didn't think.

A pang of relief reverberated through me. I snatched out toward that impression, latching on and dragging myself toward it with all the strength I had in my body. The cold bit right down to my bones, and a gasp escaped me. I flung myself faster.

My hand closed around an elbow. Firm but cold skin. My fingers skidded up it over a well-muscled arm. I tugged myself closer, and a scent like a fresh spring breeze washed over me.

Baldur. What the hell was this place he'd gotten himself into? I still couldn't see him, couldn't see anything but the awful endless dark, but I held on. I tipped my head into the nook of his shoulder, and he shifted toward me as if he'd only just noticed I was there. His arm slid around my waist. Cold. Way too cold.

I hooked my own arm around him, pressing myself against him all the way along his body. Trying to share whatever heat I still had left in my body with him. Could he literally freeze to death in this place? Everything I'd seen suggested Muninn would be pleased if her torture ended up killing us. Less hassle for her then.

"Aria," Baldur murmured, breaking through the dull silence around us. His lips brushed my forehead as he spoke. "You shouldn't be here."

"And you should be?" I said. I could feel his heart thumping in his chest now. Warmth started to flow beneath his skin where it touched mine. It had to be his memory. How could we break out of it?

I hugged him closer. "I *am* here. I'm right here with you. I don't know how you got this memory, but it's different now. You're not alone."

"I died," he said raggedly, as if the words had torn through something on the way out. "This is where you go when you die."

A realm of cold and darkness and nothing else. Oh, God. It was horrible enough for me, and I didn't thrive on light the way Baldur did. No wonder he hadn't wanted to talk about where he'd been during Ragnarok.

What did you say to someone who'd died and lingered there so long and now was having to relive that torture all over again? What could possibly convince him this hadn't been the torment it felt like? Anything I could have said caught in my throat. I opened my mouth, closed it again, and forced myself to go on.

"You survived it once. You'll survive it again. Like me. Shit happens, and we just keep going. And this time, you've got me for company. It's already warmer like that, right? All you need to do is bring the light."

He stirred against me, the flex of his muscles sending a much more enjoyable shiver through me. "I tried, but I lose it. It slips away from me."

"All right." I bowed my head back against his chest. "Then I'll just stay here in the dark with you until we make it through." And hope that would be enough.

His hand closed against my back. His head dipped down over mine, and this time when his lips brushed against my hair, the gesture felt purposeful. It felt like a kiss. My heart skipped. "Baldur..."

He sucked in a breath. I opened my eyes to a faint glow emanating from his form. He was visible now against the dark, hazing the black like one of those translucent jellyfish soaring through the depths of the ocean. Of course, I wouldn't have wanted a jellyfish to hold me like this.

Something I'd said must have gotten through. We were getting somewhere. The chilly darkness still clutched us tightly, but it was no longer complete.

"There you go," I said, looking up at him with a smile. "You found the light."

"You found me," he said, smiling back, but his expression was more tense, more present, than I was used to. The dreaminess had fallen away. "Thank you."

"I'm not sure I really did all that much," I said. "It's not exactly a painful trial to give you a hug."

He chuckled. His fingers stroked over my hair and down my back, drawing a trail of warmth through me. "That's not— I'm glad you've been with us, you know. I don't think I ever said that to you, even though I've been thinking it. *You* have a light you bring to our lives that we've needed."

I didn't feel all that brilliant, but if the god of light said it, I guessed he should know what he was talking about. And— "Hod said something like that too."

"Did he?" The soft smile came back. His eyes, even brighter than the rest of him, searched mine. "You feel close to him. And Loki too."

"Well, I did, anyway." That flippancy seemed out of

place in the moment. I didn't know what he was looking for in me. Something he needed, to break the rest of the way through this illusion? Honesty had seemed to work best before. "I like all of you. I want all of you." A flush spread up my neck saying it that openly, but it was true. "Is that a problem?"

For a second, he didn't seem to know what to say. He cupped my face, lowering his so his nose grazed mine. "Aria... I've kept my distance from the rest of the world for so long. I don't know how to be what you need. But I wish I could be it. So much."

Longing rang through his words. It called up a matching desire in me. Fuck Muninn. Fuck her stupid prison. Let her see how little I cared about *her* and her machinations. Maybe I could be the one to shatter this place. This man in front of me—he mattered. And she'd tried to break him all over again.

"You're always thinking about that, aren't you?" I said softly. "What other people need. How you can make things easier for them. Keeping us all in harmony. Maybe you should think about what *you* need, what you want, for a change."

"What I want," he murmured. He tipped up my chin, and his mouth found mine.

If Loki brought fire to his kiss, Baldur brought the summer sun. Gentle heat radiated through me, stirring up a hotter desire low in my belly. I kissed him back with all the longing I had in me, pouring that heat back into him. No chill Muninn sent could cut through this.

Baldur's breath stuttered as his mouth shifted against mine, tipping to find a deeper angle. My hands slid down to explore the panes of his muscular chest through his shirt. His fingers teased into my hair, their touch sending quivers of delight through my nerves. I kissed him harder. Drowning in the brightness of him was the most amazing thing I could imagine in that moment.

"Aria." My name came out like a sigh. His mouth traveled away from mine, charting a heated course along my jaw and down the side of my neck. One hand dropped to my waist and started to ease its way up, closer and closer to the curves of my breasts.

I arched into him with a whimper. The darkness was falling back all around us as his glow expanded. A little more, and we might be free, at least of this one place, completely. But even as the movement of his lips left me burning with need, a different sort of chill shot through my nerves.

We were going fast. This was getting dangerous. How far did I want this to go? I wanted him—oh, fuck, yes, I did—but the shadows of memories Muninn had brought far too close to the surface nagged at the edges of my mind.

I must have tensed a little, because Baldur paused. He drew back just a few inches, watching my expression. Hunger still shone in his bright blue eyes, but he said, "You know you don't have to—"

The darkness flung itself at us, battering our embrace. In a blink, it tore Baldur from my arms.

16

Aria

A fierce resolve rang through me. I was *not* letting Muninn dictate all the terms here. I'd figured her out, at least in part. We'd warmed her darkness. I could fight back.

Focusing all my energy on Baldur, I threw myself back toward him. My hand caught his ankle. We flipped through the air together and landed in a heap next to each other on cool marble tiles. The impact sent a splinter of pain through my already raw knees. The fabric of my jeans ripped, baring the scraped skin.

I rolled over. We were back in the Asgard I knew, on the main path that led between the halls, the courtyard with its fountain gleaming in the distance. Gleaming under moonlight. Muninn had brought night down over us, a dark stillness that barely unnerved me after the pitch black we'd just tumbled out of.

And she hadn't gotten her way completely. Baldur was sitting up next to me, his white-blond hair swaying as he shook his head. I'd managed to keep us together, whichever of us she'd meant to send here. I didn't see anything threatening yet, but at this point I knew better than to trust that impression.

Baldur turned to me, and his bright blue eyes widened. It was the first time he'd been able to see me properly since I'd first caught hold of him in that vast nothingness.

"You're hurt," he said. "Let me—"

Rather than keep talking, he simply scooted closer, setting his hand on the side of my knee. Even though the raw skin there was still stinging, his touch sent a flare of heat up my inner thigh.

"I can't do anything about the tear in your jeans," he said, the rough note in his voice suggesting he wasn't totally unaffected either.

"I'll take whatever you can offer," I said, and almost bit my tongue.

Baldur gave me a slow smile that looked unexpectedly wicked for a moment, but it vanished as soon as he turned back to the task at hand. With a brush of his fingers, the scrapes on my knees sealed. He took my arm, grimacing at the sight of the bruises there.

"I've been building a collection," I said.

He gave a short soft laugh. "It certainly looks like it. I can mend them at least partly."

His hand slid up my arm, more warmth flooding me with it, and not just the healing kind. I resisted the urge to nibble at my lip—the lips he'd been kissing just a few minutes ago. When he'd finished with both, his gaze came back to my face.

"Is there anywhere else?"

Fuck me, was there anywhere else I wanted him to touch? Yes and no. How about everywhere?

The thought sent another nervous jitter through me. My fingers curled against the marble tiles. Before I could figure out how I was going to answer, a muffled groan reached my ears. My head jerked around.

"There's someone else here."

We scrambled up. The city had fallen silent again, but I set off in the direction the sound had come from. Who was Muninn tormenting here—and what if they'd already been badly hurt? Baldur hurried along beside me, his steps only slowing as we ducked down a narrower passage between two closely spaced halls.

"This is..."

We both came to a halt at the end of the passage. It was the way to the secondary courtyard where we'd last found ourselves in Asgard. The courtyard where Loki had guided Hod to throw the mistletoe spear and kill Baldur in their shared memories.

The moon was low enough that only a little of its light touched the courtyard. Enough to see Baldur's corpse lying there as it had in the daylight scene. Hod was crouched next to the body, his head bowed. Dark bits scattered the marble tiles beside him. It took me a second to realize they were the snapped pieces of the mistletoe branch.

Baldur had stiffened. As I glanced over at him, he squared his shoulders. With careful steps, he crossed the courtyard to his twin.

"Brother," he said gently. "What are you doing here?"

Hod lifted his head a few inches. His gaze flicked from Baldur to me where I was coming up behind the other god. I thought his posture tensed even more than it already was. He looked to his twin again.

"The raven put me here—what do you think? Where better?"

Baldur sat down beside him, close enough that if he'd extended his leg completely he could have nudged his own corpse with his foot. "I don't see anything holding you here."

"Oh, I tried to leave. Trust me. That didn't go so well."

The strain in his voice made my heart ache. I wavered, standing a few feet away, not sure this was my moment to intrude on. It wasn't as if I had anywhere else to go, though. Maybe I'd see a chance to weaken Muninn's prison more.

"Are you all right?" Hod added, his gaze still on his twin. "I can't imagine, going through all that again... I know you don't like to talk about it, but I also know it still haunts you, the first time."

Baldur's face fell. "I've tried to set it behind me, to not let what I felt then affect anyone else now. I'm sorry if I—"

"Oh, by the Allfather, I'm not saying that you did anything wrong. Just... We've been together since the womb, Baldur. I know when something's off. And it's been off from the first moment we found our way back to Asgard." His mouth tightened. "You live like there's ten layers of gauze between you and the rest of the world— like if you soften every possible blow in advance, nothing ever has to hurt. No one who's really all right has to put that much effort into staying that way."

Baldur wet his lips and looked at his hands resting on his knees.

"Finding the truth in the memories," I said quietly. "Changing the way you all remember what happened... It's wearing away at the prison. It's helping us get out."

I knew what Hod meant about the layers of protection the light god seemed to have swathed around him. That dreaminess I'd noticed from the first moment I'd seen him, that he carried almost like a suit of armor. But right then, as he inhaled shakily, something in the way he held himself changed. His spine straightened; his jaw firmed. As if he'd willfully sloughed off a few of those layers of armor.

He'd heard me, and he was coming through to fight in his own way.

"You're right," Baldur said. "It was... Death broke me. It broke me and then broke the pieces it'd made of me all over again, and somehow they came back together when we woke up in that field in the aftermath, but I've never felt as if they quite fit the way they're meant to anymore. I suppose I've spent a long time trying to avoid acknowledging just how wrong I came back out, hoping it might turn right if I just kept up a good face for long enough."

"I'm sorry," Hod said hoarsely. "By the nine realms,

I'm sorry."

Baldur clasped his shoulder. "I never—"

The corpse shuddered. Baldur's voice cut off with a hitch. The form of his previous self, tunic stiff with dried blood, heaved itself onto its knees. Blood flecked the dead god's lips and teeth too. The corpse's eyes were clouded over, an icier blue than Baldur's real ones had ever been, but they focused on Hod. Words rattled from its throat. "Do you think sorry is enough, brother?"

Oh, God, what horror had the raven come up with now? The actual brothers threw themselves to their feet, stumbling backward to where I stood. Hod stared blindly toward the corpse, his muscles rigid from head to toe. The thing heaved onto its feet and swayed. A putrid sour smell like decaying meat rolled off it, making me choke.

"Draug," Baldur murmured, his expression tight.

"What?" I said, taking another step back when the corpse lurched toward us.

"Something like your idea of zombies," Hod said with a rasp. "The dead come back to life. Bloated and rotting and looking to pass on that death."

His hand balled into a fist, but I knew just looking at him that he'd never hit that thing, no matter that it obviously wasn't his brother in any way now. The real Baldur had never risen from the dead like that, clearly. Muninn was mixing memories again, merging that death with monsters the gods had dealt with.

The creature raised its arm. It was clutching the mistletoe spear, reformed, the pointed end stained dark red and aimed at Hod. "You struck me down, you stole my life and my light, and you want to say you're *sorry*?" the draug warbled.

Hod flinched. Baldur gripped his forearm. "That's not me," the light god said. "Those aren't my thoughts. I —" His jaw clenched. "Maybe I hide that from myself too. Maybe I've been angry at you. Maybe some part of me didn't want to talk to you because then you might have been freed from the pain too. But that wasn't fair of me. I'm the god of justice, and I *know* you didn't deserve that. I know you never would have meant to hurt me."

"But I did," Hod said. "I *killed* you. It was my fault, at least as much as Loki's."

"All your fault," the draug gurgled. "All your—"

It lunged unexpectedly, swiping out with the mistletoe spear. I'd been right about Hod. His arm shot up, but only to block the blow. The spear tip sliced across his wrist, drawing a thin red line. Panic flashed across Baldur's face. He might have been able to stop it too, but God, how could anyone ask him to kill *himself* after all the horror he'd been through.

Desperation wrenched through me. The draug would kill Hod if it could. That was what Muninn wanted here.

It heaved forward with another lash, and I thrust my hands toward it. "*Stop!*"

Lightning crackled through my veins and burst from my palms. The corpse jerked and seized. It toppled over and hit the ground, disappearing into a puff of dust.

I lowered my arms, my body trembling. I really wished I had a little more control over when that happened, even though I was pretty happy with this outcome. I shot a glance toward the twins.

Baldur gave me a terse nod. A ragged sigh rushed out of Hod. He rubbed his face.

"That thing and what it said might not have been real," he said, "but you have to know it was my fault. Who else can you blame?"

The light god glanced at me and swallowed audibly. "If it'll take truth to beat Muninn's prison: How about myself?"

Hod's head jerked up. "What in Hel's name are you talking about?"

"I was there, wasn't I?" Baldur waved his hand toward the middle of the courtyard. "I let Mother collect those vows. I let them play that game—which was stupid; Loki was right about that. I flaunted the care and security I'd been given. If I'd been happy simply having it, if I'd shut down the idea of the game... I never would have been in a position where anyone could have hurt me. I can take responsibility for that."

Hod stared at his brother—as much as he could stare. A little of the tension left his shoulders. "So where do we go from there?" he asked.

Baldur dragged in a breath. "Well, I think first we need to get out of this prison. But then, after... I'd like to be able to talk to you about it more. Darkness is your forte. Maybe you'll be able to help me make more peace with what I went through. If you don't mind taking on some of that burden—"

"Of course not," Hod said quickly. "Anything I can do. It won't be a burden if it helps you heal."

A small but bright smile spread across Baldur's face. "Then I couldn't ask for anything else, brother," he said.

Hod smiled back—and the courtyard around us shimmered. It was working. I froze, my heart leaping as I searched for the chinks in Muninn's construct. We'd challenged the memories she was using again, shaken up her foundations. There had to be—

There. I caught a glimpse of gray rock through a gouge in the tiles. I leapt toward it, and the world tilted over again.

No. My arms darted out. I trained my mind on that image, that rock, the reddish glow and the ashen smell I'd caught before. That was the real world. That was the place we needed to reach.

The courtyard whirled away in a gust of fog. I half dashed, half skidded through it, my feet bumping over rough rock. A scene stretched out ahead of me, hazy around the edges like the moment I'd seen of Muninn and that man in what had seemed to be their home.

But this was no house. A dark cliff loomed over me, and a tall figure strode along several feet ahead of me, beside a river that glowed searing red. The figure wore a faded cloak and a broad-brimmed hat. A familiar twang ran through my chest.

"Odin!" I started to call, but the name snagged in my throat. As I'd opened my mouth, a flurry of ambermonsters rained down on the god from the cliffside and from crevices in the ground beside it. He swept out his spear, but it was knocked from his grasp in an instant. He crumpled under the mass of attackers.

"There," Muninn's sweetly hoarse voice said, somewhere distant. "I delivered him. I fulfilled my end."

"You did," a man answered in a searing tone. "But are *you* really finished with him, raven?"

A force socked me in the gut, sending me flying back into the fog, and I lost her answer.

17

Hod

The warmth in my brother's voice melted some of my anguish. I smiled at him, sensing exactly where he stood from the gentle energy he carried with him everywhere. It seemed to wrap around me, quiet but reassuring. Were we really good? Better than we had been, at least?

Ari sucked in a startled breath. Her footsteps dashed across the tiles, and my head snapped around to follow them. The air rippled around us. I stepped forward instinctively. If she'd seen some sort of danger, I had to be there for her too.

For one instant, I thought I heard the rustling of a cloak, a rough cough I would have sworn was my father's. My breath caught. Then something struck me, walloping me off my feet.

"Hod!" Ari's voice called out from somewhere far

away. Fear lanced through me. I reached after her, but I was sliding, tumbling, farther away.

I fought the wind, but no movement I made affected my direction. It blasted me so hard my ears rang. I careened through formless space until I jarred with a halt at the edge of a thin rug across a cool stone floor. My hand braced against the polished surface.

The raven's illusion had started to shatter. That must be it—I *had* gotten a glimpse of Odin, of some other place that wasn't part of her construct. Ari had been right. As we changed the way we thought about our memories, what we knew to be true about the past at all, Muninn's hold on us weakened.

And because we'd gotten close to breaking through, she'd tossed us away again.

At least I was gone from that awful courtyard. What worse was there she could throw at me?

It wasn't myself I should be worrying about now, I didn't think. What she'd put Baldur through—every part of me ached just remembering the way he'd talked about it. How broken he felt. How *wrong*. If she put him through that again, how much longer could he hold himself together?

Or maybe he was stronger than I was giving him credit for. Even as an ache rippled through me, a sense of relief flowed beneath it. I'd finally closed the distance that had grown between us. He was opening up to me. He was willing to ask for my help, even though those conversations would be even harder for him than for me. If I could pull him even a little out of the haze he'd been hiding in, all the torture I'd faced here would have been worth it.

Where had Muninn sent him now? What had she done with Ari?

The raven had already battered our valkyrie so much. I hadn't even had a chance to make sure *she* was all right, to ask what she'd been through. I'd been so lost in my own pain. But if Muninn had dredging up those memories for me and my twin, twisted them so cruelly... My stomach twisted at what she might have thrown at Ari.

I had to try to find my way back to her. She'd managed to find me before, using the connection between us. Whenever the prison faltered, it was because we were working together, finding those truths together.

I filled my lungs, getting a sense of my surroundings. A wide room, from the air currents drifting past me. A streak of warmth fell across one of my shoulders where sunlight must be spilling through a high window. A subdued murmuring carried through that window, along with the rasp of dragged logs.

My body tensed all over again. Ah. Muninn hadn't thrown me far in time from my last location. They were building Baldur's funeral pyre out there.

A wail rose up, petering out into sobbing. Nanna, Baldur's wife. I swallowed hard. I'd heard, after we'd all returned, that she'd thrown herself on his pyre to be burned up with him. You could almost say I'd killed two gods when I'd killed him.

Some *had* said that.

If this was that day, then I was in one of the lower

chambers of my father's hall, one I'd never had reason to be in before then. The door behind me would be locked, until—

The bolt thudded over. The hinges squeaked faintly as the Allfather stepped inside with slow footfalls. Heavier than usual. I could feel the slump of his shoulders in the sound of his exhale.

Other footsteps slipped in behind him, so faint I might not have noticed them if I'd had all my senses to distract me. The second visitor stopped at the edge of the room and set the object he'd been holding against the wall with a soft thump.

"My son," Odin said.

"Father," I replied. Anticipation had clamped tight around my chest. I stayed turned away from him, turned toward the window and the sun. The first time, when this had really happened, I'd been standing facing him, hadn't I? But there was no need to recreate this memory perfectly. Would he say the exact same things, make the same excuses?

Part of me clenched with grim satisfaction at the idea of him having to speak to my back to deliver this message.

"You know, if it were simply my choice, we wouldn't be here," Odin said. His voice was strained but resigned. He'd already decided he had no choice. "But the balance is needed, now more than ever as summer fades from this realm. We need dark as well as light, but darkness when light is gone cannot be sustained."

"I know, Father," I said.

I didn't really. He'd been afraid of Ragnarok's approach; that much had become clear. But the balance hadn't made any difference to that war. It had come down on Asgard anyway. Had this one act really swayed anything that mattered?

I hadn't thought it through in much detail in the original moment. I'd been drowned in my own guilt and grief. His pronouncement had stung, but in some ways I'd welcomed it. Death was better than living on with the knowledge of what I'd done. I was accustomed to darkness. I could accept it.

Now, I could have tried for the door, tried to push past him, but I found I couldn't bring myself to move. What were the chances I'd make it that far before he and his companion stopped me anyway? Maybe his words would make more sense this time around.

"If we don't appease Asgard's sense of rightness a little longer, we could lose everything," my father went on as if I hadn't spoken. "That is the burden we bear."

He came forward to stand beside me where I was kneeling. His hand rested on my shoulder. "If I had known it would play out this way…"

Then what? He'd have done something differently? What *had* he seen, in all the travels he'd been on, in his visits to the Norns, in his searching visions? All of us knew that the Allfather saw more with his one eye than anyone else came close to with two. He'd sacrificed the other so that he could glimpse what lay beyond the world of the present.

"I would have liked to at least bear witness at the funeral," I said. "Pay my last regards." As if this conjured version of my father would give me any satisfaction there.

The stranger by the wall spoke up then as he hadn't

in reality. His voice was a low rumble. "The blind god bearing witness? The murderer giving regards to his victim? What a joke."

"Quiet," Odin boomed. His grip on my shoulder tightened. "I think it is better for all of us if the deed is done before then," he said to me.

Better for *all* of us? A jolt of anger shot through me. I heaved myself to my feet and turned to face him after all.

"Why don't you just say it, Father?" I said. "Instead of talking about deeds and balance. You're going to kill me, like I killed Baldur. That's the plain fact of it. Shouldn't all this dancing around it be beneath you?"

With each sentence that spilled from my mouth, the anger inside me flared a little hotter. A good burning, with a sear of energy and conviction. So much more than I'd even realized I'd kept bottled up.

The Odin drawn from my memories was silent for a moment. Then he said, "Perhaps it is. I simply thought it might be kinder to you to avoid that much bluntness."

"Kinder to me?" A sharp laugh tumbled out. A starker searing blazed through me, so fast I didn't have time to examine it before the words burst from my mouth. "Tell me the truth, Father. If I'd been the one who'd died first—if it'd been me falling at Baldur's hand— would you have sacrificed him? Your light, your joy? Would our mother have even let you?"

The questions left an acid aftertaste on my tongue. Odin stood still and silent. Every moment he didn't speak turned any shame I might have felt at asking him back into anger.

"Are you just not sure?" I demanded. "Or is it that you know I won't like your answer if you tell the truth?"

The stranger by the wall started to laugh in a rolling cackle. Odin stirred. "What answer would you want me to give you, my son?" he said in a low voice. "What could I say that would satisfy you?"

Those words punctured the vicious swell inside me. It was my turn to hesitate. A tremor ran down through my gut.

How long had I wondered those things without saying them, without even really thinking them? The emotion in them felt very, very old. Bone-deep and woven through my veins.

How many times had I watched the other gods, including our parents, gravitate toward Baldur while leaving me alone? When had our mother ever gone on a quest to protect *me*, to ensure I'd never come to harm? It had all been for Baldur. Baldur the kind. Baldur the just. Baldur the bright.

Why wouldn't everyone prefer his company to the dark god who was most at home in the night?

Loki's cutting remarks in the courtyard came back to me. *The bitterness was wafting off you like the stink of a skunk.* Maybe it had been. Because this wrenching sensation inside me wasn't just guilt or grief. Some part of me had been desperately jealous of the love that had been extended to my brother, over and over, and not to me.

I gritted my teeth, but I couldn't stop that final question from rising up in my mind. Had I wanted to hurt Baldur, deep down? Wanted to let him fall, just once?

"I don't know," I said to my father. "I just— This isn't what I wanted. I know this isn't what I ever would have wanted."

"It's easier to make our choices again in hindsight," the Allfather said. "That doesn't mean you weren't true to yourself when you made them."

"He's my *brother*," I said, but the protest came out weak even to my own ears. Nanna's sobbing carried through the window, along with the fainter sounds of weeping from other gods. All that grief, I'd brought to this place. Because I'd resented how happy Baldur made them?

Odin clasped my shoulders again. He bowed his head close, brushing a dry kiss to my forehead like a blessing, the way he had all those centuries ago. "It's time. I swear that I will see you, after."

"Father..." I didn't know what else to say.

Odin stepped back, a whisper of his feet against the rug. The stranger lifted his club off the floor and approached with weightier steps. His clothes rustled as he raised his arms. I braced myself, my hands clenched at my sides.

Even if I was bitter, even if I'd been jealous, I could take my death with honor. I could accept the punishment I was due. I—

I wasn't really supposed to be here. I'd taken that punishment already, ages ago. This was Muninn's doing. If I got swept up in the memory, I could die here all over again. That was what she meant for me. She'd wanted me to get swept away until I forgot to defend myself.

The air shifted as my executioner swung his club. I dodged to the side, a split-second too late. The heavy shaft of wood missed bashing open my head, but it did clock me across the temple.

Pain exploded through my skull. I staggered backwards, reeling, and tipped over an edge in the floor into freefall.

18

Aria

This time Muninn's intent hurled me upward—up, up, into a darkness that spilled open to clear blue sky. As it spat me out, I whipped out my wings to catch myself on the breeze.

I whirled around. I was hovering over Asgard, the gleaming rooftops scattered below me, alone.

No, not alone. A brown feathered body soared past me. Freya's falcon, beating her wings hard as if her life depended on getting wherever she was going as quickly as possible.

I swooped after her, straining to keep up. "Freya!" I called. "What's happening? What's wrong?" Was this one of her memories now, a chase by a monster maybe? I didn't see anything flying after us.

The falcon didn't slow. "Freya!" I called again. What

if it wasn't her after all but a construct of her? But when I stretched my senses, I could feel a tingle of her godly life energy even from a few feet behind her.

I flapped with a fresh burst of speed and shot past her. If she was caught up in a memory, maybe I could snap her out of it like Loki and I had before.

"Freya, can you at least give me a sign—"

The falcon banked at the sight of me. With a flutter, the goddess slipped out of the falcon cloak, draping it across her shoulders to keep her body in the air. She stared at me, her eyes slightly glazed as if she wasn't totally seeing me yet.

"My daughter," she murmured. "I have to find my daughter."

My heart squeezed. "Freya," I said, grasping her hand like I had when she'd thought she was slipping back into old age. "I don't know what happened before, but Muninn wants to hurt us. To break us down. If it freaks you out this much not being able to find your daughter, I don't think she'll ever let you. But you did find her eventually, right?" I had trouble believing Loki would have joked about bartering her off to giants otherwise, but then, I'd have had trouble believing he'd have orchestrated a murder too, so what did I know?

Freya's breaths smoothed out. She swiped her hand across her eyes. "So you bring me back to reality again, Ari," she said with a crooked smile.

"I've needed those reminders too," I said, thinking of the bedroom in Petey's foster home, Hod's strained voice.

"I just... I saw her. But you're right. This is what

Muninn wants—us frantic rather than trying to work our way out." The goddess sighed. "Let's go down to earth. I'll think clearer there."

We had flown past the main city and the orchard now. Freya dipped down toward a glade in the thicker forest. We came down on the soft grass near a large stone well. Brown ridges jutted from the soil at the edge of the glade, but their shape and texture looked wrong for rocks. After a moment I realized they were enormous tree roots. But where was the tree?

"Those are the roots of Yggdrasil," Freya said with a tip of her head. "I suppose the raven decided no harm could come from us having access to them." She let her hand trail along the edge of the well. "This is where the Norns used to pass their time. They liked to water the tree, among other things."

Other things. "I've heard you and the others mention the Norns before," I said. "I've got no idea who they were."

"None of us really did," Freya said. "They just turned up in Asgard one day and settled down here, these three. Spinning prophecies. Some said they determined the future. I think they merely read the signs to see where it was leading." She paused. "Odin did too. We weren't married then, but I noticed he visited them often. He's always wanted to know all he can about what is and what will be."

"I guess that habit got him into a lot of trouble this time around."

"So it seems." She shook her head with a wry expression, her golden hair tumbling over her shoulders.

"I wouldn't have stopped him from his wanderings, even if I could have, though. I miss him when he's away, but that thirst for knowledge is part of what makes him the man I love."

I thought of the Odin that Muninn had shown me in her tarnished Valhalla. He hadn't looked all that loveable then. But then, Freya could obviously be bloodthirsty too. That was why they got along.

"You've been together a long time?" I ventured.

"His relationship with the twins' mother fell apart not long after that scene you saw with the mistletoe and so on," she said. "I wouldn't have thought of anything happening between us, but after Ragnarok, when we all got our second chances... It seemed foolish to hold back from what might make us both happy."

She glanced at me sideways, with a teasing lift of her eyebrows. "I notice you're indulging in at least one godly dalliance of your own."

My face flushed. The worst part is, I didn't even know which god she was definitely talking about. Probably Loki. She'd definitely seen him kiss me.

"That's just—" I started, and didn't know how to finish that sentence. I had no idea what I was doing with any of them. Only that it felt good when I was doing it, and at the time that always seemed like enough. The thought of trying to define anything, put some sort of meaning on it, made my stomach twist.

"It's all right," Freya said. "You'll find no judgment here. I get the impression you're a woman who knows how to protect her own heart. I expect you can handle them."

Them. Okay, she'd definitely noticed something was up with the others. This seemed like a good time to change the subject.

"Muninn stayed with Odin for a while after Ragnarok, didn't she?" I said. "You must have gotten to know her pretty well back then. Maybe something you saw back then will give us more of an answer to escaping this place."

"I don't know if I would say I knew her well." Freya leaned back against the well, her expression going thoughtful. "She couldn't shapeshift back then, you know. She was always a raven. An extraordinarily intelligent and aware raven, but she could only speak to Odin, through a mental bond they had. I never spoke with her directly. From the way he talked about her, though, he thought of her as an old friend. I never got the impression he saw reason to doubt her loyalty."

"Did he ever say what happened right before she left? Where she'd gone? If there was anything—"

Before I could finish the thought or Freya could answer it, the walls of the well blasted apart. One of them knocked me back into the darkness that filled the gaps between Muninn's constructs. I sucked air into my lungs, trying to right myself, and only tumbled backward again. The wind whirled me around and then dropped me.

Muninn didn't want me asking those questions. Okay. I must be getting close to tearing this prison down.

I landed on a scuffed wooden floor, my hand shooting out to grip the banister instinctively. Freya was gone, off in some new nightmare of her own, no doubt. The dreary smell of my mother's house closed in around me. Tension clenched around my chest.

The upstairs hallway. I was in the upstairs hall, outside the bedrooms. Even as I realized that, steadying my feet on the floor, the creak of the stairs carried up from below. A heavier creak than my mother's steps would have made. Every muscle in my body clenched up.

"No!" I shouted at Muninn, wherever the hell she was. "Don't you dare."

Another creak. My heart lurched. I hurtled myself toward the wall at the end of the hallway with the burn of all my valkyrie strength.

"Let. Me. *Out.*"

I slammed into the wall fists first, and it cracked apart with a shower of dust. With a heave of my feet and a frantic flap of my wings, I propelled myself into the darkness on the other side.

Muninn's wind whipped around me, yanking me to the side. Not back there—no, I wouldn't let her. I beat my wings as hard as I could against it, groping for anything else I could hold on to. I'd beat her before. I could be stronger than her if I just pushed hard enough.

A forest spiraled by beneath me. The invisible force walloped me to the right. As my head spun, Asgard's halls flashed by. Was that Thor outside one? I reached toward him, but the wind snatched me back too fast, too strong.

I spun head over feet. "Ari!" Loki's voice called, there and then sucked away in the howl of air around me. I jerked up and plummeted, tripped down a set of steps— the ones from my old elementary school?—hurled myself upward again, and caught another impression of one of the gods. There. I wanted to go there. We'd fight her together. I was so done with being shoved around at the raven woman's whim.

My wings ached, but I flapped them even harder. The force dragged at them—and then snapped. I tumbled headlong into a dark room, landing on my ass.

A cold stone floor lay beneath me. A sliver of a moon gleamed beyond the window, and a massive bed stood just across from me. Three figures clustered to my right, huddled together by the back wall. And one form, pale and lean with short black hair mussed as if the wind had dropped him here not that long ago, bent over the bed.

Hod didn't seem to have noticed me. His hand drifted over the covers—over the body lying under them. A halting rattle of a breath carried from the pillow, followed by a faint groan. Hod's mouth tightened. He drew his fingers to his palm, and the sensation echoed in the shadows that lurked inside me as he pulled the last shreds of life into his own darkness.

The room had been quiet before, but now the hush was total. Hod straightened up, his hand falling to his side. His head turned toward his audience, and they pulled even farther back without a word. His lips curled into a grimace. He headed out the door, and the watching figures let out their breaths in one combined exhalation.

I pushed myself to my feet and hurried after him. I nearly collided with him in the hall outside, where he'd stopped, I guessed at the sound of my steps. He caught my elbow, steadying me.

"Ari?"

His voice was terse, but his grip on me trembled. I knew the dark god well enough to have noticed that he always got more prickly when he was trying to cover his own discomfort.

"The one and only," I said with a lot more cheer than I felt. Anything was better than my childhood memories, and at least I wasn't alone. We had a chance to escaping when we could work with each other. Muninn was jerking us around more and more. It must be getting harder for her to maintain any one illusion.

My gaze caught on an angry purple-red splotch on the side of Hod's forehead—the side that had been turned away from me before—and my body tensed. "What happened to you? Who did that?" Because I'd like to give them a matching bruise as payback.

Hod's hand rose to his temple as if he'd forgotten the injury. "It's nothing," he said, still terse. "I got careless. My skull is still intact, which is about as much as I could have asked for."

I wasn't so sure about that, but he clearly wasn't in the mood to discuss the trouble he'd encountered. I forced myself to look away, considering the hall. "What do you think we've gotten ourselves into this time?"

He shrugged. "If you saw me in there, it's already over."

I glanced back toward the bedroom. "You were taking that person's life." Person? These stone walls had an Asgardian vibe. "That *god's*?"

"Not everyone in Asgard looked after themselves so well after the rebirth," Hod said. "A few got to the point where what life they had left was barely life at all. They wanted their final end to be as peaceful and quiet as possible. So they'd call on me." He turned his face away. "This was *my* life, while Asgard was still active: called for duties no one wanted to even mention by the light of day."

Duties no one else could have done the same way, I wanted to point out. But I'd seen the way his audience had cringed away from him. I couldn't change his mind by lying.

"What now?" I said instead.

"I don't know. I suppose we wait and see what Muninn stirs up next."

Was she watching us now? Did she even realize where I'd gotten to in her ever-expanding prison? She must have to focus her attention on the others part of the time. I'd broken out of the last memory she'd tried to trap me in—I'd managed to find my way here to Hod.

"I think she's tiring out," I said. "She wants us anxious or upset all the time... It's easier to control us that way? So, maybe we'll have a better chance of breaking out completely if we're somewhere with happier memories. I haven't seen your hall yet. Why don't you invite me over?"

Something that sounded like a guffaw sputtered out of the dark god. "I don't know how happy that place is, but all right. Will you accompany me home, valkyrie?"

"It would be my pleasure," I said in a formal tone, and the corners of his mouth twitched upward.

We left that house behind and made our way to a smaller hall of stones that looked a slightly darker gray than the ones around them. A craftsman with a sense of humor or Hod's own choice? He nudged open the door and strode over the threshold, confidence drawing his posture even straighter in the familiar space.

"Here you have it," he said dryly. "Home sweet home."

19

Aria

My pulse thumped with curiosity as I peeked through the closest doorways of the dark god's house, finding a dining room and a parlor with a single chair and shelves upon shelves of books. So very Hod. Were his texts here written in whatever the Asgardian version of braille was, or did he have to use magic to read like he did with his collection back on Midgard? He trailed along behind me, but he didn't speak, letting me take it all in uninterrupted.

The lonely chair niggled at me. "You lived here alone?"

"Live, present tense, when we're back in the real Asgard," Hod said. "Does that surprise you?"

"I don't know. Maybe it was silly, but somehow I figured you and Baldur were pretty inseparable."

"Oh, he has his own hall, closer to the main courtyard. I'm told it has a beautiful view."

A strange edge had come into his voice. That talk with his twin had seemed to dull some of the guilt he'd been feeling, but not enough, apparently. Was that a point I could press to widen the gaps in Muninn's prison?

"We're going to get out of here, you know," I said. "And then you'll have all the rest of your godly lives to hash out anything else that needs hashing out. At least—"

I caught myself, realizing just in time that my own thoughts had started to veer in a guilty direction. Hod didn't need my pain layered on top of his own.

But clearly he knew *me* too well at this point. "At least I can talk to him?" he filled in quietly. "At least he's still here. At least he remembers who I am."

"It's stupid to compare," I said. "Let's just stick with, I know how shitty it feels when things aren't right with someone you care about that much."

"There might be some day, when all this is over, that you could talk to Petey again."

I stared at him. "You'd *let* me, Mr. Leave All Your Earthly Concerns Behind?"

Hod rubbed his mouth. "Maybe I've gotten a very thorough example of why trying to simply forget about old hurts isn't always the best course of action. And... even *I* know it's not right that he doesn't even remember you, all the things you did for him, when you could be a real part of his life." His voice dropped even lower. "I'm sorry I had to add to your pain."

My throat tightened so suddenly it took a moment before I could speak. "Hod... I'd have been in a lot more pain if I'd had to leave him with my mom. Or anywhere else the dark elves might find him. You were helping me."

"In a way." He leaned back against the door frame. "That's how I contribute, isn't it? Through darkness, through taking away, through death... Even *Loki* brings brightness rather than quashing it sometimes."

"Okay, now you're being ridiculous," I said. I'd have needed to argue with him even if I hadn't thought challenging all our takes on any given situation was the key to getting out of here. "You contribute a lot more than that. You've got all that knowledge from those books, and you're probably the closest thing this group has to a voice of reason, even if that's a little pessimistic sometimes, and... and sometimes what you take away is pain. You gave me the space to talk about things I didn't think I ever wanted to talk about with anyone. To let some of it out, knowing you were listening, knowing that it mattered to you. That meant a lot."

"You've only seen a small fraction of who I am, valkyrie," he said, but his voice had softened a little.

I made a scoffing sound. "I've seen enough. So you're not all shiny like Baldur and you don't have Thor's bravado or whatever. So what? You're *all* so different from each other... It's kind of hard to imagine you all not being together. Like you've got the perfect balance between the bunch of you."

Something about that comment made Hod wince. "Not quite perfect," he said. "There were all those fault lines we were trying not to let crack open. But with you being here—you've made it easier somehow. Stirred things up just enough to start clearing out the tensions, I suppose. It's hard to imagine *you* not being with us now."

A giddy warmth passed through me at that comment. I stepped closer to him, taking his hand.

"You know, I watched what happened in that courtyard, and I don't think you can be blamed for what happened. You didn't know. You thought you were just joining in with the rest of them. Loki—"

Hod shook his head with a jerk. "I'm not so sure about that," he said roughly. "Some of the things the raven has reminded me of... There were times I felt so *angry* at how the gods favored Baldur. I didn't have to throw the stick that hard. I could have asked what Loki was up to."

I squeezed his hand harder. "Do you really think you wanted him *dead*?"

The dark god paused. His jaw flexed. "No. Never that. But I might have wanted him to hurt just a little, just once. To have one thing go wrong."

Oh, my dear dark god.

"I don't know," I said. "That sounds pretty normal to me. I loved Francis with all my heart. But there were totally times when I resented all the things he got to do that I couldn't because he was older. And times, after the really bad stuff started... when I hated that I had to go through that and somehow he got off free. Emotions aren't fair. They just are. Does that mean it's my fault he died?"

My pulse hitched as I said it, as if I were half afraid Hod would say yes, it was. He brought his hand to my face, stroking his thumb across my cheek. "Of course not," he said firmly. "That's hardly the same, though. And I doubt *Baldur* ever feels jealous of anyone. The light in him just washes away anything like resentment."

"Didn't you hear him before? He's been angry too."

"Only briefly, and for justifiable reasons."

"Hmph." I tipped my head against Hod's chest. His fingers moved to my hair, sending pleasant shivers over my scalp with each caress. "I'd bet being good all the time is stressful in different ways. Can't you just believe you're good enough?"

"Can't you?" he shot back.

"I'm working on it," I said. "You have helped me in lots of ways, you know, despite all the grimness and skepticism. I think it says a lot that you could be so kind to someone you didn't trust at all to begin with."

Hod was silent for a moment. His hand stilled against my hair. "I don't think you can call those acts kindness, Ari," he said. "That was a man falling in love with you."

My breath stopped; my spine stiffened. I pulled back from Hod to stare into his face. His expression had already tensed.

"It's all right," he said raggedly, backing up a step. "I didn't expect the sentiment to be returned. If it's easier, you can pretend I never—"

An ache shot through my chest, even starker than my panic. I moved automatically, grabbing the front of his shirt and yanking him back to me. Bobbing up on my toes at the same moment to capture his mouth with mine.

With a stuttered breath, he was kissing me back. His lips had the same salty, softly smoky flavor as the scent that clung to him, and they moved against mine as if he knew exactly how to find the most sensitive angle. As if he'd charted every inch of me a hundred times instead of this only being our second kiss.

The sensation sent a quiver of joy through me, but the quiver turned into a tremor after just a few seconds. I clutched his shirt, trying to lose myself completely in the heat of his mouth, but I couldn't get control of my body.

Hod eased back, not so far this time. His forehead brushed mine. "Ari?" he said hoarsely.

I burrowed my face in his chest. "I'm sorry," I mumbled.

He paused. "Do you want to tell me about it?"

Just like that. Just like he'd asked when I'd randomly burst into tears on him outside my mother's house not that long ago. Simple and straight-forward and opening the door to anything I could have had to confess. No pushing, no pressure.

This was kindness, no matter how you looked at it. Did he really think it mattered why he offered it?

"I haven't let myself feel much about anyone other than Petey in a long time," I said, still talking to his shirt. "It was always safer to keep my distance. So much easier not to get hurt that way. I don't... I don't really know how to do it anymore. How to care about people. How to fall in love. But you all are so... I can't help caring. I can't help *wanting*. And it fucking terrifies me. So it's not you—it's not you at all. It's just me being a mess."

"You're not a mess," Hod said, outright fierce now. He tipped my head to press a kiss to my forehead that somehow felt as passionate as the meeting of our lips a few moments ago. "I'm not asking for anything. I don't expect anything from you. Whatever you want to give, whatever you can—"

His head jerked up. Before I could ask him what was wrong, I felt it too. A shift in the air around us, as if a breeze that shouldn't exist had passed straight through those stone walls. A breeze with a smell of chemical ash. Our talk had shaken something loose.

The breeze was coming from the doorway. We both dashed into the hall at the same time. The walls rippled before my eyes. I backed up and threw my shoulder at one, ready to grab Hod if the illusion broke completely.

My shoulder thumped against it with a spasm of pain. The wall didn't even crack. I frowned.

"Maybe we can get the memories to shift while her focus is shaky," I said. "Think of someplace else, someplace you'd rather be."

Hod's jaw set with concentration, and almost immediately the world whirled around us. The breeze that washed over me was sweet with the smell of spring grass, and when I blinked, I found we were standing in a spartan bedroom that held an ebony frame bed and a matching wardrobe, the plaster walls a light mint-green. I might have been confused if I hadn't recognized the view out the window.

"This is your bedroom in the house on Midgard?" I said.

A thin blush colored Hod's cheeks. "I wasn't really thinking," he said quickly. "It just happened to pop into my head."

I spun around and found myself faced with a blank wall where the exit should have been. "Muninn managed to steal the door." But I could get more of a running start at this one. I threw myself forward, fists slamming out.

My hands rammed into the wall. A gasp broke from my mouth at the impact, but it held. I swiveled, rubbing my knuckles.

Hod was already moving to the window. He jerked at the base and heaved again, but it didn't budge. The glass only rattled when he smacked his elbow against it.

"She lost some of her control over the construct, but she's got enough to keep us in here," I said. "Shit."

"We're getting closer," Hod said. "I could really sense the world outside that time. Have you found anything else that affects her focus?"

When had the prison shifted, either against Muninn's will or because she seemed frustrated with me before? Usually when we'd been talking, breaking down the memories the construct was based on. But also sometimes when I'd gotten too close to knowing more about her. And sometimes...

I stepped right up to Hod. "Let's see how closely she's watching."

I traced my hand up his chest to slip around his neck. Hod's distant eyes darkened with desire. He lowered his head, meeting me halfway in between.

As he kissed me, it was hard to remember I'd started this to try to shake up our prison. I didn't know what to do with all the things Hod had said, all the emotions churning inside me, but every inch of my skin ached with wanting.

One of his hands came to rest on my waist, the other sliding around my back to tug me a little closer. He kissed me again, shadows bleeding from his body to shimmer across mine. They licked the corner of my jaw, over my collarbone, across my ribs, sparking of bliss everywhere they touched.

I teased my tongue across his lips and they parted. The heat of his mouth soaked into mine. A pang shot straight through my core. Oh, hell. I couldn't walk away from this.

"I think her attention must be elsewhere," Hod murmured against my lips with another caress of shadow.

"Good," I said, my heart thumping. "Then we can do this."

I pulled him with me toward the bed, claiming another kiss as we went. He groaned. I clambered onto the mattress, up on my knees so we were almost the same height, and he slid his hands up under my tank top. His thumbs stroked the lower curve of my breasts and the shadows he brought caressed over the top. I wasn't sure whether he was directing them or they just came of their own accord until one whispered across my back—and flicked open the clasp of my bra.

"Hod," I said, momentarily startled.

"Do you mind?" he murmured. "I can call them back. My powers—when my feelings are this heightened—"

"No," I said with a quick shake of my head. "Don't stop. That was *hot*."

He chuckled. "Not something I've usually been accused of being."

"Not an accusation," I muttered in return. "Take a compliment." The last word cut off in a whimper as he cupped both my breasts, stroking my nipples into instant peaks.

I shoved my hands up under his shirt, eager to explore him skin to skin in turn. My touch drew a hungry sound from his lungs. He tipped me over on the bed, coming to rest beside me, his lips sliding down my neck.

Hod kissed my throat, my shoulder, my sternum, as if he were worshiping every part of me, leaving no inch of my skin unadored. Then his head dipped lower. His mouth closed over the tip of my breast, and I moaned, gripping his hair. His shadows teased over my lips, others tracing down my spine. I arched against him, wanting so much I couldn't find the words to say it.

He lifted his head for a second, and my pulse skipped with the thought that he was going to nudge me onto my back. But he just ducked lower, trailing kisses down the center of my chest to my belly. His shadows darted along the waist of my jeans as he flicked open the button. He tugged them down, his breath grazing hot against my panties.

His next kiss, right above them, was so tender that my throat choked up. I gripped his shoulder, tugging him back up, afraid of what might spill out of me if I let him keep going in that direction.

Hod came without complaint, tucking his arm around me and kissing me hard on the lips. My bare leg hooked over his thigh. Another groan escaped him, reverberating around my moan. His erection pressed against my core as he kissed me even harder. His shadows licked against me like an echo of a hundred tiny kisses, and the emotion I'd been trying to hold in tight spilled out anyway.

My chest hitched. Hod eased back from the kiss. He traced his hand down the side of my face and paused at the corner of my eye.

"Are you *crying*?" he said, his voice raw.

I sucked in a breath and just barely managed not to sob. "Good crying. Happy tears. I'm just... It's our thing, right? You've got to have me in tears at least once or it's not a full conversation."

"Ari..."

I tucked my head against his jaw. "I've never been with anyone and had it really mean anything before, okay?" Even that roll-around with Loki, as much as I'd enjoyed it, as many of my rules as I'd been breaking by going through with it, had been about scratching an itch, chasing desire, nothing all that much deeper.

No commitments. No proclamations.

But Hod had already made one.

His tone softened. "Ari. My valkyrie." His fingers slipped to my chin. He tipped it up so we were face to face, gaze to blind gaze. "I love you," he murmured, sounding a little choked himself.

I yanked his mouth back to mine. As our tongues tangled together, I wrenched at his slacks. He kicked them off, and I palmed his erection through his boxers. He held me tighter, pouring himself into the kiss. A wave of bliss coursed through me.

One of his shadows wriggled under my panties to lick against my clit. I gasped, gripped by a deeper need. "Please."

We fumbled our way out of our underclothes together. Then the smooth skin of his rigid cock was gliding against my clit. A wave of pleasure coursed through me. I hooked my leg back over his hip and urged him right into me.

A cry escaped me as he filled me. The giddy burn expanded from my core through every other nerve. Hod clasped my thigh, thrusting deeper as we fell into another kiss. We rocked against each other side by side. His shadows teased over my breasts, tingled against my clit. I whimpered, my teeth scraping his lip, and he bucked into me faster.

My head tilted back, my eyes rolling up. Hod took me deeper still, with a ripple of shadow all across the most sensitive points of my skin, and I came with a moan and a shudder. His breath turned ragged. He thrust with a few more erratic jerks of his hips and followed me into that final bliss.

20

Aria

I clung to Hod, reveling in his heat and his sweat-damp skin pressed against mine, until the afterglow started to fade. He kissed me, so sweetly it sent a fresh wave of longing through me. But I knew we didn't really have time to relish this moment. My gaze slipped to the window.

"I wish we really were back in this house," I said. "I wish..."

"A lot of things?" Hod suggested. His arms tightened around me for a moment. "Me too. But we'll get out of this. I can't imagine anyone keeping you caged for long, valkyrie."

I had to nuzzle him again, my mouth finding his for one last kiss. "Next time no crying, I promise," I said.

A smile crossed his face at the mention of a next time.

Hod was always handsome, like all the gods were, but when he smiled... I couldn't look away.

I sat up and fumbled my bra back into place. My jeans and panties lay in a tangled heap near the foot of the bed. I squirmed into them with a glance around the room. "I'm not sure getting it on helped us much in the way of getting out of here, sadly."

Hod muffled a laugh with his hand. "Maybe if we tried again right now," he said with an uncharacteristically playful gleam in his eye.

I stuck my tongue out at him, even though he couldn't see it. "Don't get a one-track mind on me. Let me see—"

I hopped off the bed—and right through the floor.

Apparently our hook-up had affected Muninn's construct after all. The wooden boards gave way beneath me with a sigh. I plummeted down into darkness with barely time to let out a squeak.

My wings shot out from my back automatically. I whirled around, trying to grab hold of something, to fly back to Hod.

"There you are," Muninn's voice murmured as if inside my head. "Thought you could hide away? Here's something you should see."

An unseen force threw me against a stone wall. I slid to the ground in a low-ceilinged cave. The scent of rot filled my nose. I flinched, bracing myself against the rough stone.

I knew this place. It was Nidavillir, where I'd first come looking for Odin—the home of the dark elves.

The thought had only just crossed my mind when a

woman tumbled into the cave through an opening I couldn't make out. The same opening I must have come through. She landed on her hands and knees, chestnut waves falling across her face, wings just like mine flexed above her back—and several dark elves hurtled out of the darkness to fall on her.

I clapped my hand over my mouth to cover a cry as one of their knives sank right into the other valkyrie's skull. Blood gushed out around it, painting her hair even darker. She crumpled to the ground. One of the dark elves spat on her before wheeling his short stout frame to stalk away.

"That's what happened to the others they sent," Muninn said. I had the impression she was perched just above me, even though there was nothing really there to perch on. "That's what your gods sent them *to*. Off to do the hard work for them, off to the slaughter."

"Only because the gods couldn't get to Asgard themselves," I said, closing my eyes against the sight of the murdered valkyrie. "They *would* have come themselves if they could." Freya's anguished voice rose up in my memory, talking about how much she wished she could go for her husband.

"And then they summoned you up." The raven woman's voice was disdainful. "And you followed the trail too well. If you'd just let it go, not tried quite so hard, I never would have needed to shut them away."

"Oh, so now this is *my* fault?" I shoved myself to my feet and spun on my heel, but I still couldn't see her. "You want to talk about taking responsibility for your own problems—how about you take responsibility for the shit you've thrown us into?"

"My offer still stands," Muninn said. "It won't for much longer. Do you really want to see how much worse this can get?"

"It'll only get worse for you, you—"

I raised my fist, and the force of her illusion smacked me across the head. I stumbled backward through the cave wall where I was whipped around and tossed to the side. My gaze leapt across the darkness, searching for some sign of Muninn.

A flicker of an image passed by my eyes. The raven woman hunched on a stone ledge, her head in her hands, her hair hanging lank through her fingers. A murmur slipped from her lips. "So damned tired of this."

My hand snatched out, and the image whisked away. I couldn't have said whether it was a glimpse of the present or the past. Whenever it had been, Muninn had been faltering. I felt her in that moment, her emotions radiating through the space around me. She was nearly exhausted.

A spark of triumph lit in my chest for about two seconds. Then I was hurled to the floor on the same stained carpet I'd found myself skidding onto what felt like days ago. The sour-stale odor of my mother's house wrapped around me, thicker this time. Thicker than I thought it'd ever actually been in reality.

Oh, no. We weren't doing this again. I sprang to my feet and heaved myself at the wall, meaning to break straight through it the way I had in the hall before.

My shoulder jarred against the solid plaster. I almost tripped over my feet landing back on the ground, holding my arm.

Muninn wasn't letting me go that easily this time. However exhausted she was, she'd been ready for that trick. But she couldn't be ready for everything. I just had to keep pushing.

The door. That was how I'd gotten out of this house the first time. I swung around toward it—and my mom appeared in the mudroom doorway. She planted her hands on her knobby hips.

"Sneaking out again? Can't be bothered to give your own family the time of day anymore, can you? I don't know how I raised such a selfish brat."

My chest clenched up. I didn't want to hear this. I *really* didn't want to find out what it might lead to. Jerking around in the opposite direction, I dashed for the other doorway.

She was already there in the kitchen, hunched over a chipped mug of coffee. "I'll do the laundry tomorrow," she muttered. "You can wear those pants another day. No one's going to be sniffing your ass."

I darted past her to the front hall. A different voice, a slightly flat tenor, carried from behind me. "Ari? Won't my favorite little lady spend some time with me?"

Trevor. I remembered those times way too well. The pat of his hand against the sofa cushion. The too-eager gleam in his eyes. The way he'd sit a little too close his knee pressed next to mine. The movies he'd pick—not porn or anything, but with more sex and violence than any other parental figure would let a nine-year-old watch.

I'd known from the first time he'd called me over that something wasn't quite right. He just hadn't shown me how wrong he could get until a year later. All I'd known then was that when I'd refuse, he'd vent to Mom, and Mom would lay into me even harder.

My pulse scattered. I ran toward the door—but there wasn't any door. Just one of those damned blank walls.

I didn't slow down. No, I sped up. I hurtled forward and rammed into that wall with a heave of my valkyrie strength.

My body slammed against it and toppled backward, pain radiating through my bones. My breath came out in a gasp.

"Ariiii."

The stairs. Maybe I could fly from a window. I swept around the bannister and charged up the creaking steps. Mom's bedroom. Muninn wouldn't be thinking about that. I'd barely ever gone in there.

I pivoted at the top of the stairs, leapt for her door, and Muninn's guiding force battered me across the head as if I'd been hit by a cast iron frying pan.

I fell, and fell, not onto the worn boards of the hall floor but into a thin mattress with a bulging spring by the small of my back. A scratchy wool blanket was pulled over my body up to my chin. The bedroom lay dark and silent around me. A cricket chirped outside.

A heavy footfall sounded on the stairs. One creak, and then another, and then another. Panic blared in my head. I moved to push myself off the bed and found myself paralyzed.

Just like I'd always been back then. Frozen with fear and dread, sweat beading on my forehead as my heart hammered at my ribs, listening to him climb those stairs.

Only this time Muninn must have had a hand in this, pushing me down.

The blanket glued me to the mattress as if it were a layer of cement. A wave of fatigue trembled through it, but she held me there with all her strength. I'd be willing to bet she wasn't paying attention to anyone but me right now. She wanted her vengeance for the ways I'd challenged *her*.

Do you really want to see how much worse this can get?

I couldn't even open my mouth to curse at her. My jaw stayed clamped tight. Outside my bedroom door, the stairs stopped creaking. Trevor padded across the hall.

Fucking God, no no no *no*. I squeezed my muscles against the paralysis, but I couldn't budge an inch. More sweat trickled down the side of my face, leaving a chilly path in its wake. I willed my wings to emerge, to propel me off the mattress, but they stayed locked inside me. My lip pinched as my teeth bit down on it. The pain didn't jar me loose either.

The door eased open with a soft squeak. Trevor's broad, gut-heavy form stood silhouetted on the threshold. He stepped inside and closed the door behind him. Under his breath, he started to hum that damned song, that stupid fucking song about daisies and sugar that had been all over the radio for months and still made me want to vomit when I heard it.

Back then, I'd have squeezed my eyes shut. Pretended I was asleep, that I didn't know what he was doing, couldn't feel any of it, couldn't care. Maybe if I gave him nothing, he'd get bored of the groping and the rutting against my pajamas.

Except it hadn't worked. He'd gotten more creative as time went on. Oh, please, no, let this not be one of those times. Let this at least be early on, when it was easier to shut out.

He ambled across the room and stopped at the side of the bed, beaming down at me with that sickly crooked smile. This time, I glared back at him as if I could throw him out of the room with the power of my horror. My body cringed beneath the blanket.

He bent down to grasp the corner, and another figure emerged from the darkness right behind him. Hands clapped, and my mom's former boyfriend burst into flames.

The flare of the firelight glanced off Loki's light red hair and pale face. His amber eyes seemed to flare too as he watched Trevor crumble to the ground in a heap of dust. He kicked at the smoldering pile with a sneer. Then he turned to me. "I came as fast as I could. I'm sorry he got that far."

I snapped upright and in the process discovered that I could move again. A sound almost like a whine emerged from my throat as I scrambled off the bed, swiping at my arms as if the itch of the blanket and the memories that came with it might follow me. My shoulders were shaking.

"Ari..." Loki extended his hand and then paused with it halfway between us. Not knowing whether I'd want whatever comfort he was planning to offer, I guessed. I didn't know either. Another shudder wracked my body.

Control. I had to get control of myself. I still had to get *out* of here.

"Thank you," I managed to say, stiffly but steadily. "I... Thank you."

Loki nodded, his gaze fixed on mine. His hand still hovered in the air between us. He shifted his weight as if to move toward me, and the stairs creaked again.

I froze, my stomach flipping. Another creak, and another. He was coming *again*. Another Trevor. Fuck, no.

Panic took over. Before Muninn's invisible force could shove me back down on the bed, I bolted for the door.

21

Loki

Ari's distress radiated off her as if she were in full nuclear meltdown. I'd been able to feel it thrumming through the ever-shifting walls of Muninn's prison, growing sharper and more frenetic as I'd tried to follow our thread of connection to her. Now, watching her dash from the bedroom into the hall, it wracked my nerves.

So much pain contained in that small body. If she'd just talk to me, let me help her fight it...

I hurried after her. There was no way I was letting her out of my sight now. Muninn could throw a thousand walls up and I'd outpace them all to stay with our valkyrie. She'd needed me in there, and she'd need me again. Whether she liked that idea right now or not.

Ari swerved in the hall toward one of the other doorways, but as she ran for it, the floor dropped beneath her feet like a trap door opening. She dropped through it with a yelp. Cursing, I dove after her.

We landed in her kitchen, kitty-corner around the Formica table. On the other side of the room, a teenaged boy with a head of messy blond waves like Ari's was attempting to stare down a middle-aged guy who was a few inches taller and several wider, with a bald patch at the back of his head he'd inexpertly combed over.

It took me a second to recognize him in the glare of the kitchen's lights. Bald Spot was the man I'd just fried in Ari's old bedroom.

"You get out of this house, and don't you even *think* about coming around here again," the boy was saying, his voice ragged and his face flushed red. "If you ever touch her again—"

"You don't know what you're talking about, kid," the man said. "That girl makes up all kinds of crazy stories. Whatever she told you—"

Ari made a wounded sound. "No. Francis. *No.*"

She shoved herself around the table and reached for the boy—for her older brother—but this once Muninn wasn't building with solid matter. Maybe she needed to preserve her energy, or maybe she saw it as a new form of torture. Ari's hand passed right through her brother's arm. He kept talking at a desperate pace as if he hadn't noticed her at all.

"She didn't tell me. I found proof. I know what you did, you sick fuck. So if you don't get the hell out of here, I'll—I'll call the police."

The man had tensed, but he kept his voice even. Even and dark. "You don't want to do that, Francis. Do you have any idea how they'll treat her if you feed them some story—"

"It can't be any worse than what you did to her," Francis snapped back.

Ari cried out and lunged at him again, but she caught hold of nothing but air. Her brother threw himself at the man with fist raised. The man dodged to the side, slamming out his arm to deflect the blow and shoving back at the same time.

Francis careened to the side, his head hitting the sharp corner of the counter with a fleshy crack. A sob broke from Ari's throat. She dropped with her brother as he collapsed, blood flowing from the wound on his head.

"Ari." I bent over her, touching her shoulders, but she smacked my hands away.

"Leave me alone. You don't— Francis..."

She pawed at his head as if she could heal the wound with strength of will alone. Muninn had let him turn solid now. Blood streaked across Ari's palms. My gut twisted, but for once in my long existence I hadn't the slightest idea what to say that might be welcome, that might soothe her anguish even a smidgeon.

He was lying there... lying there like Baldur had. Pale and bloody and totally innocent. I closed my eyes against the image.

By the Allfather, how could she have reacted in any other way to that scene in the courtyard? The crime I'd committed echoed one of the most horrifying moments of her life, only this time with me in the role of villain. I was lucky she was even tolerating me in the same room as her.

I might not ever be able to fix this. She might not ever

forgive me for one act committed ages before she'd even been born.

That knowledge sank heavy in my chest. All right. That was a fact. But it was also a fact that I wasn't in the habit of giving up just because a situation looked dire. If there *was* a way to fix this, to repair the wreck I'd made of whatever we'd had, I'd damn well find it. Especially if in doing so I also struck a blow against this damned prison.

After a few minutes, Ari sat back on her heels with a stuttered sigh. She swiped at her face with the back of her hand.

"It's not him," she said to herself. "It's not him. It's Muninn's idea of torture. But she can't really hurt him." She raised her head and shouted at the ceiling. "I'm not falling for this!"

The body deflated with those words. In a matter of seconds, there was nothing left of the supposed Francis except a smear of dust. Even the blood on Ari's hands crumbled into dust. She swiped them against her jeans and stood up.

"We've tired her out," she said to me. "She can't keep anything up very long anymore, not without all her concentration. And it's not worth it if it's not working. Not torturing us." She shot another glare at the ceiling with that comment, just as a woman appeared in the doorway.

Ari's mother. They weren't that close a match, but I could see Ari's heritage in the narrow gray eyes, the slant of the woman's nose. The corners of her mouth dug deep as it curved into a scowl.

"You had to go and ruin everything," she said, jabbing a finger at Ari. "We were fine. Just fine."

Ari's fingers clenched against the table-top. She took a step backward. "No, we weren't."

"You never could be satisfied with the way things were. Always had to make everything about you. As if any man would look at a scrawny thing like you and want *that*."

"Shut up."

"Francis would still be alive. I'd still have Trevor. We were making a real life for ourselves and you took it all away. If you'd just kept your stupid mouth shut—"

"I did, you fucking bitch!" Ari yelled.

Her mother froze, as if even this construct of Ari's memories didn't have a response to that. I was willing to bet Ari had never screamed like that at the real one, however much her mother had clearly deserved it. That moment's hesitation did give me an opening, though.

I held up my hand, a surge of heat racing through me. "Permission to light her up?"

Ari's jaw tightened, but her lips curled into a grim smile. She nodded with a short jerk of her head.

I snapped my fingers, and a spurt of fire shot up from the floor to engulf this figure of her mother.

Like the man upstairs, the construct crumbled before it even really started to burn. Not the most satisfying vengeance.

Ari sagged against the table, but her shoulders stayed tense. Her gaze lingered on the doorway. Braced for some new horror to emerge.

The moment stretched. Nothing else appeared.

Muninn had switched to torturing my fellow gods for a bit, I had to guess. Or else she was even more tired than Ari had suggested—too tired to do more than hold these walls in place.

"You should never have had to see that again," I said into the silence. "Muninn deserves to have her head shoved up her ass and pulled right back out of her neck for putting you through it."

Ari's lips twitched at my creative imagery. She pushed away from the table. "Why are you here?"

"I'm trying to look after you, as difficult as you seem intent on making that task."

Her gaze snapped to meet mine. "Who says I need looking after?"

"I think we all do in this warped place, don't you?" I cocked my head. "It doesn't matter what you think of me, pixie. You're *my* valkyrie. I'm the one who dragged you into this mess—which has turned out to be a far bigger mess than I anticipated, unfortunately. So, even if you've decided to hate my guts, I'll still be here to burn up any assholes who need burning." I waggled my fingers in the air.

She let out her breath. "Yeah. They did need that."

Her head drooped again. I swallowed, but curiosity wriggled up my throat anyway. One of the milder of my many flaws.

"She really blamed you like that, didn't she? Your mother? Muninn didn't just make that up."

"My mom... lived in a reality where nothing much mattered except that nothing could ever be her fault." Ari lifted one shoulder and dropped it in a half-hearted shrug. "In a way she was right. If I hadn't been here, if I'd been better at hiding it, Francis wouldn't have died. Trevor wouldn't have gone to jail. Everyone would have been happier."

My jaw set against another flare of anger. "Everyone except you."

"Well, I didn't count, in her equation. I really didn't tell, you know. Two years, and it kept getting worse, but he'd always say, if I said anything, I'd be the one who got in trouble. I knew who my mom would believe. I knew Francis couldn't really do anything, not without ending up in the line of fire too..." Her voice wobbled.

"It isn't your fault," I said sharply. "Don't you dare take on one speck of the guilt that piece of human excrement should be carrying."

Her head jerked up again, her eyes startled. Did it really surprise her that I was angry about this? I didn't know every detail of what that bastard had done, but I'd seen enough in that scene and in every reaction Ari had when anyone got close to her...

"I could burn him up for real, you know," I said abruptly. "When we're out of here. An inexplicable case of spontaneous combustion. Really it'd be a kinder end than he deserves." But so very, very satisfying.

Ari's gaze stayed on my face for several seconds. "No," she said finally. "I don't think that would actually make things better." She looked away, braced against the edge of the table. "If I'd just fought back, if I'd screamed and hit or found some other way to show him he couldn't get away with it... But he could. He probably sized me up and knew I'd be too weak."

She sounded so defeated in that moment that my rage burned through me twice as hot. "You weren't *weak*," I said. "You were a child in a horrible situation. Trying to protect yourself and your brother like you always do. Taking it all on yourself so no one else had to be hurt. You were so fucking strong that even when the worst thing possible happened, you got through it, you kept going. You didn't let that despicable woman crush you. You didn't let the past break you."

"But maybe I did," Ari said. Her grip on the table tightened. "You don't know... It's been ten years since I last saw that asshole, and I still haven't managed to get him out of my head. I can't completely relax with anyone; I can't completely trust anyone. No commitments, no risk that I'll get hung up on the wrong guy, because it feels like it'd be so easy to end up trapped like that again."

"Ten years isn't that long after trauma like that," I said. The bitter weight I carried under my rage twinged in agreement. Centuries and centuries sometimes weren't enough.

She shook her head. "You don't even see it. You... You were the first person I've hooked up with who I knew I couldn't just walk away from the next morning. The first person in *ten years* where I didn't already have one foot out the door. And I fought it; I didn't want to take that chance, because I knew I wasn't going to want to walk away."

My heart squeezed. And then she'd ended up trapped in here with me, finding out just how wrong I could be. She'd given me that trust...

"So, why did you take the chance?" I asked quietly.

Her shoulders rose and fell. She glanced at me sideways. "I felt like you understood. You understood, and it didn't stop you from wanting me."

"It still doesn't," I said, not that hooking up was very high on my to-do list at the moment. I'd have been happy simply to have her welcome my embrace, to let me take a little of the burden she'd been carrying too long. "I've seen all that, I've heard everything you've said, and I still think you're one of the strongest human beings I've ever met, Ari. I wouldn't even recommend many gods take you on."

The edges of the room shimmered. I went still, watching from the corner of my eye. Muninn's constructs were becoming even more fallible. Maybe it wouldn't be long before we could shatter them completely.

"*I* don't understand," Ari said, turning to face me. "How could you have done that to Baldur? To *Hod*? You put both of them through so much shit—you murdered Baldur and made Hod feel like he was the murderer..."

My stomach clenched into a ball. I kept my voice even. "I never lied to you. I told you I was a villain. I'm sure the others told you plenty too. I am what I am, Ari."

Her gaze didn't waver. "If you're such a villain, then why are you trying so hard to help me? I have trouble believing it's just to get into my pants again."

"No one's ever that black and white. I'm allowed my finer moments."

"So, why didn't you make that one of your finer moments?" she demanded. "You had a choice, didn't you? Were you really just so pissed off at the stupid game that you thought murder was the answer?"

Despite my intentions, I bristled. "It was a lot more complicated than that. You saw one fragment of the history. I had my reasons."

"Then tell me them, instead of all this garbage about 'I am what I am'!"

My stomach clamped tighter. "That's the truth," I snapped.

"Is it?" she said. "Or is it just easier to avoid answering the question if you claim you're a bad guy and wash your hands of everything else?"

The accusation struck deeper than she could have realized it would. I managed to contain my flinch. If she'd known, if she'd had any idea...

But wasn't that just how she'd been arguing with me about her supposed weakness?

The walls around us wavered, more obviously this time. Ari's eyes widened. She pushed off the table, taking a step toward the cabinets. Then, with a heave, she threw herself forward with a smash of her fist.

The cabinets, the counter, the wall collapsed inward into darkness. Ari let out a cry of victory. She was just swiveling toward me when a gust of wind blasted up between us and tossed her right into that void.

22

Aria

Lord help me, I was so sick of being tossed around. As I spun into the blackness, I focused all that frustration on my memories of a sweet yet hoarse voice and a flutter of dark wings. Where was Muninn? Where was she, so I could punch her in her little raven face? She'd thought showing me all that history would wear me down? It'd only made me even more eager to tear her down—one feather at a time, if that was what it took. We were almost there. I *knew* her strength was flagging.

My wings flapped and banked. The darkness shifted around me, and I was back at the cage I'd seen Odin in before.

The Allfather was slumped against the iron bars, his head bent to the side and hat drooping low. His presence reverberated through me. The ring of fire continued licking at the base of the cage. A more muted reddish glow seeped over the rock all around—a cave. This was a cave somewhere.

I turned. A wall of thick liquid flowed past what I guessed was the cave's entrance, emanating a red-hot light like the stream where I'd seen him ambushed.

Like... magma? Were they keeping him in a *volcano*? After everything I'd seen in the last few weeks, it didn't seem impossible.

Muninn's voice drifted from deeper within the cave. "You never thought I was capable of something like this, did you? You never thought very much about me at all, except for what I could bring you. Did you even wonder where I was, all this time? Did you assume this place had killed me, not that it clearly mattered to you much?"

"I knew where you were, Muninn," Odin said, his voice low and rusty. "You didn't appear to want to be disturbed, so I let you be."

That sounded like a kind enough answer, but from Muninn's sharp inhale, it'd somehow made her angrier.

"I had a life," she said. "A life I could have had for all that time before. I used to think—"

"What?" Odin said after a moment, shifting against the bars. "What did you think, my raven?"

"I'm not *yours*," she spat out.

I edged away from them, away from the cage, toward the fall of magma. There was a small gap between the gush and the rock. If this was the entrance, if I could see more from here, maybe I'd have a better idea where we could find Odin... whenever we were able to really go looking for him again. If he was even still here.

My foot scraped the rough stone floor. A curse echoed through my head from some other place. Then a force battered my face with so much power I had to close my eyes and raise my hands to shield myself.

I stumbled backward and spun around, not wanting to accidentally take a dive into that searing waterfall. The uneven ground flipped up beneath me.

That next journey was nothing more than a brief lurch. I dropped my hands and found myself back in the front courtyard of Asgard, crouched on the marble tiles where we'd first arrived. From the slant of the sunlight and the deepening blue of the clear sky overhead, it was evening. The same time it'd have been if we'd never left this spot? I didn't have any clear sense of how much time had passed in Muninn's prison, traveling through all those years of memories.

The breeze licked over me with just a hint of a chill. I straightened up. The soft warbling of the water cascading from the central fountain was the only sound. Nothing and no one else stirred in the vast city of the gods, anywhere that I could see.

I hugged myself, wavering on my feet. Was Muninn just waiting to spring some new horror at me? Of course, if she'd wanted to horrify *me*, she wouldn't have sent me to a place I had no memories of. When I'd ended up back in some version of Asgard before, it'd always been to join one of the gods in a painful replay of the past. Was she so worn out she couldn't even bother to come up with a new torture for me?

Where were the other gods, then? Should I go

exploring? Or try to bash my way out of this place into wherever they were?

I'd just made up my mind to at least peek into a few of the nearby buildings when the air shuddered. With a grunt, Thor came tumbling into the courtyard beyond the fountain as if out of nowhere.

He hit the tiles shoulder first, just barely protecting his head with the back of his arm. Mjolnir thumped against the tiles beside him. A pained sound escaped the thunder god as he rolled onto his back. I ran to him, my heart thudding faster when I saw how he staggered a little pulling himself onto his feet.

One side of his shirt was stained with blood. *His* blood, it had to be, because all the rest had turned into those smears of dust that marked my clothes too.

"Ari!" he said with that broad smile, even as he clamped his hand against his wound.

My breath hissed through my teeth. "Sit back down," I said, grabbing his other arm. "What the hell happened to you? Where did she send you?"

He didn't exactly listen to me, but he did lower himself onto the stone rim of the fountain, the water in the pool rippling with the impact of his brawny body. He glanced down at his bloody shirt and grimaced.

"Better idea," I said. "*Lie* down."

"I'm fine," he said stubbornly.

"You're about to refill the fountain with your blood," I shot back. "There's nothing dangerous here, not yet, anyway. And when something does show up, I have the feeling you'll be better at taking it on if you haven't been ignoring a mortal wound."

Thor frowned, his shoulders flexing. My throat tightened. "Please?" I said.

That one word softened his expression. He sighed, but he lay back on the rim. I peered over him, realized there was no way I was reaching the water by leaning, and hopped right into the pool.

Thor winced when I splashed a little water on his side to wash the wound.

"Can you get your shirt off without making it worse?" I asked.

He raised an eyebrow at me. "You want my shirt."

"So I can try to bandage you up!" I said, giving him a firm look.

He chuckled and wrenched at the fitted tee on the other side. With a quick yank of his muscled arm, the fabric split from hem to sleeve.

I helped him peel the shirt off, careful around the wound, which I could now see was a wide but shallow scrape across his lower ribs. The bleeding looked to be slowing. I tied together the pieces of shirt as well as I could and wrapped them around his torso with a thicker set of folds over the scrape.

Thor lay back down when I was done. I sat on the fountain rim by his head and squeezed as much water as I could out of my jeans.

"It was battles," Thor said, answering my earlier question about where he'd been. "Battles, battles, and more battles. I didn't realize I had so little variety in my life, but it seemed like that's all the raven could come up with out of my memories."

"And one of those battles got the better of you?"

"Not exactly." He paused. "I got tired of all the bashing and battering. Thought maybe I could try a different strategy. Why not? She was shifting the memories all around. Who was to say I couldn't? So I tried calling a halt to the battle to have a calm discussion about why exactly we were fighting. Because I've got to tell you, I didn't have any idea by that point."

I nudged his hammer, which he'd laid on the ground beside him, with my toe. "Thor the Thunderer gave diplomacy a shot. Not what she was probably expecting. And?"

He scowled. "They didn't even stop running at me. I waited to see if maybe, if I didn't even fight back, that might change something, but..." He motioned to his side. "So much for diplomacy."

"Well, it's not really your area anyway, right?"

He was silent for a longer moment this time. "I'd rather it was. But I guess this is what I am."

The comment echoed Loki's excuse so closely I had to restrain a cringe. But Thor had told me before how uncomfortable he felt realizing how much of his life had been made up of violence. He'd seemed to think I'd see him as some kind of beast because of it.

I let my fingers brush over his dark auburn hair, displacing the strands that had come free from his short ponytail. "That's just what she wants you to think," I said. "I'd like to see *her* give diplomacy a try."

He rumbled in agreement. "Should I be coming up with my last words?"

"No, I think you're going to survive. It looked worse than it was."

"Oh. Well, in that case."

He shoved himself upright, ignoring my squeak of protest. With a sweep of his arm, he scooted me into his embrace. He kissed my temple. "I'm glad you're all right, Ari. I kept thinking... You *are* all right, aren't you?"

I thought of all the horrors I'd been wrenched through, mine and others', in the last several hours, and my stomach knotted. But Thor hadn't been part of any of that agony. It felt like a relief to tip my head against his bare chest, soak up his body's heat, and say, "Yes. Yes, I am."

I didn't want to move. I wanted to stay there with his hand stroking up and down my back for a good long time. I was tired too. The smell of him, like warm tangy mead, teased around me. Without thinking, I found myself pressing a kiss to the bulge of his pecs just below his collarbone so I could taste it too.

Thor's fingers shifted against my back. "Ari," he said in a voice low with hunger—and a thud sounded behind us.

I leapt up, Thor heaving himself onto his feet almost as quickly. Freya was just straightening up where she'd fallen near the edge of the courtyard. Her golden hair was in disarray, but she somehow smoothed it perfectly into place with one brisk flick of her hands.

"Well," she said, with slight shudder. "This has been... something."

Baldur emerged from the air several feet away from her, managing to land on his feet. His youthful face looked weary, but less pained than when I'd found him in the darkness. I hoped Muninn hadn't found anything worse to torment him with.

His sweeping gaze caught on my hasty bandage around Thor's side in an instant. He strode toward his brother. "You're injured."

The thunder god waved him off. "Ari took care of it. I'll live."

"I might as well do what I can while we have a moment." Baldur's bright blue eyes darted to me for a moment, looking me up and down as if to confirm I hadn't taken any new beatings since he'd last seen me.

"I'm okay," I said quickly. "Take care of him."

As Thor started grumbling something about not needing to be taken care of and Baldur knelt beside him, the air twanged again. Two more figures emerged at opposite ends of the courtyard almost simultaneously: Hod and Loki.

Hod caught himself with a knee and a hand on the tiles and scrambled up, summoning his shadowy cane with a flick of his hand.

"It's all right," I called to him. "So far everything's been calm here."

His shoulders relaxed at the sound of my voice. "I tried to catch you when you fell," he started.

"I know," I said before he could try to apologize. "She had a few more tricks up her sleeve."

Loki strolled toward us, taking in the courtyard with his amber gaze and a curious tilt of his head. "I wonder what tricks she has in store for us here. All six of us, back where we started. An interesting choice. Who got here first?"

"I did," I said. "And then Thor. It hasn't been that long, though. Maybe half an hour?" If I could rely on my sense of time at all. "I guess she's run out of horrible memories to throw us into. All that tossing us around really tired her out."

"We didn't break as easily as she was hoping," Hod said grimly.

"And it's easier to keep us all contained if we're in the same place?" Freya suggested.

"So she might hope," Loki said with a sly smile. "I'm all for disappointing her once again. Ari, you still seem to be the key to cracking through these constructs of hers."

He made a beckoning gesture, and I stiffened automatically. His expression darkened, just for a second.

Hod stepped toward me. "You don't get to order her around," he said. "And I'm not sure I'd trust any plans *you* come up with anyway."

Loki let out his breath in a huff. "Come on now. Do we really need to act as if the past really did just happen? We've coexisted peacefully for ages before now. Do I need to list all the impossible situations I've extracted us from before?"

"No," Hod said. "I let what happened go to keep the peace for too long. We're all thinking it. I'll say it. However we get out of here, after this, you're not welcome anywhere near the rest of us."

Loki's jaw worked, but he kept his tone glib. "I hardly think you can make that decision for the entire party. Declared yourself the voice of the group since you can't be the eyes, have you?"

"Loki," Baldur said, his voice melodic but steady. He

left Thor, turning to face the trickster. "I think you've done enough."

My pulse skittered. This was starting to sound like more than just the bickering they'd done before. "Wait," I said. "None of this matters unless we do get out of this place. We get out, and then... and then anything you need to decide, you can decide it then." Fighting with each other was only going to serve Muninn's purposes.

Hod shrugged. "I've already said my piece."

"Well, fine," Loki said with a dismissive sweep of his hand. "As if the two of you didn't fall in with us in the first place because no one else could stand being around constant grimness and the perpetual daze. Thor and I will just have to go adventuring again."

He cast an expectant glance toward the thunder god. Thor shifted his weight. "When we do get home, I think I'll be happy to stick to feasting and drink for a good long while."

"I guess you'll have to enjoy those adventures on your own," Hod said. "Just don't bring them back here."

"*Here*?" Loki replied, his tone sharpening. "You mean this prison we're still stuck in, which apparently you've all forgotten—except Ari, of course?"

"Anywhere," Hod snapped back.

"Okay, just *wait*," I said, stepping between them with my arms outstretched. "This is what Muninn wants. We have to work together, try to understand each other—it's by looking at the past in different ways that we've started to bring down her prison. We can talk this through."

A blaze had already lit in Loki's eyes. It seared through his voice. "It doesn't sound like we can. So you'll cast me out, finally, after all the ages, because of one act over a millennium ago? I suppose that's Asgardian justice for you."

"One act that left the two of them dead," Freya put in tentatively.

"Do you think I *enjoyed* that fact? Do you think I delighted in that outcome?"

"Yes," Hod said. "By all appearances you did."

"By all— You can't even *see*— You weren't even here to know—" Loki threw up his hands.

"Maybe you'd better go now," Baldur said softly. "When we break the prison, we'll all get out, either way."

A tremor ran through the trickster's body, so sharp I half expected him to explode into flame. His eyes narrowed.

"*No*." He spun around, jabbing his finger at one and then another of them. "No. I'm done. Let's have a real look at the past and see just how very different it is from the picture he painted for you. I've kept that bastard's secrets for his benefit and *yours* for long enough. Ragnarok was supposed to be the end. I was done with this fucking role. But you all just can't help shoving me back into it. So, here you go. I'll be your villain one more time."

"Loki," Thor said warily. "What are you ranting about now?"

"You'll see. Or hear, as the case may be." Loki shot a fiery look Hod's way. He motioned to the sky. "Play along with me, little raven. You wanted Odin to fall? Let him fall even farther. Let's have the tower. Let's have that night. You can see the memory. Isn't it juicy enough for you?"

For a few seconds, nothing happened. My heart pounded in my chest. I was just opening my mouth to try to salvage the mess we'd made of this meeting when the halls upended all around us. The tiles bucked up, throwing us toward the sky.

23

Aria

My wings shot from my back. I caught hold of Thor's hand, the closest of the gods. Then stone walls thudded into place all around the six of us.

We jolted to a stop on a woven rug in a cylindrical room. The ceiling rose to a peak overhead, crisscrossed with rafters and shadows. Windows ran in a circle all around the room. A tall wooden armchair that looked as if it'd sprouted right out of the floor stood in the center. There was no other furniture except a few small tables and bookshelves beneath the ring of windows. A cold night breeze rippled past us, carrying a scent like a coming storm.

Lightning crackled across the sky outside, followed by a distant rumble of thunder. The hairs on the back of my neck stood up. I didn't like the feeling of this at all.

Thor squeezed my hand. Baldur took a step toward the chair. He stared up at it, wide-eyed.

"This is my father's tower," he said. "The Allfather's high seat. I've never seen it."

"Because he never invites *anyone* up," Hod said from near my other side. "No one enters the tower except for Odin."

Thor bent close to me. "From that chair, through those windows, it's said he can see anywhere in the nine realms," he murmured.

"He never invited *you*," Loki said to Hod, that fiery heat still flaring in his eyes, crackling through his voice like the lightning outside. "No one sets foot in this room except the Allfather—and his closest collaborator."

"And that's you?" Freya crossed her arms over her chest, sounding skeptical.

"Do you really think Odin brought one of the treacherous jotun into Asgard, swore a blood-bond with me, just for fun? Surely you know him better than that."

"Why are we here?" Thor said. "What's so important that we had to see?"

Loki spun around. "You want to hold the Allfather up on a pedestal? You want to be horrified at the things I've done? Everything, all of it, was for *him*." He spat out the last word.

Freya's eyebrows drew together. "What in Hel's name are you talking about?"

"Let him tell you!"

Loki flung his arm toward a figure that had just stepped out of the shadows. Odin swept his broad-brimmed hat from his head and set it on top of one of the low bookcases. He ran his hand through his grizzled brown hair.

It wasn't the real Allfather. Even if I hadn't known he couldn't be here, that Muninn would never let him free from his cage just for this, my valkyrie nature didn't respond to this form's presence with the same tug of recognition.

No, this must be the Odin of Loki's memories.

And no one else but Loki had been here in those memories. Odin nodded to the trickster as if he'd expected to find him in the room, his gaze skimming right over the rest of us. "Oath-brother," he said in his low dry voice. "It's good to see you."

Loki's attention had completely shifted to the Allfather. He propped himself against one arm of the great chair. "Is it?" he said. "You didn't seem all that pleased with me when we last met down below." He gestured toward the city beyond the tower's windows.

"You know how it goes," Odin said. "We need a sense of order."

"While you're encouraging chaos behind their backs."

"Now wait a—" Thor growled, stepping forward, and Loki jerked up his hand to stop him. He was playing out the conversation of the past, I guessed, but this was still his present self, fully conscious of both us and Odin.

"You wanted answers," he snapped at the thunder god. "Watch and you'll get them."

I tugged at Thor's arm, even though a nervous ache was forming around my gut. "I think we need to see this," I murmured.

Thor drew back beside me, his mouth set tight. At my other side, Hod stood stiffly. His blind gaze was low, but I could tell that every particle of his attention was focused on the scene in front of us. Near the other side of the chair, Baldur and Freya stood silent and tensed.

The construct of the Allfather was shaking the dust from his cloak. "It's not chaos I've asked of you," he said. "Stir emotions. Spark passion. Start the flames burning."

Loki rolled his eyes at Odin. "You and your damned poetry. Spark a passionate desire to see my head on a pike is about the size of it."

Odin paused and turned fully toward the trickster. "Are you unhappy with your situation?" he asked. "When we met, when I offered you a place here in Asgard, you remember the oath you took."

"I swore my loyalty to you with my blood," Loki said. He ran his thumb across his slender palm. "You didn't tell me how much that loyalty would require."

"I haven't asked much of you before now, have I?" The Allfather arched one thick eyebrow. "You've had the run of the realm of the gods. You've gotten to play your games and work your tricks."

"While nearly every god and goddess out there still treats me like I'm an evil stowaway in their midst."

"And that's exactly why you're the one for this role."

Loki's hands clenched at his sides, the knuckles turning an even starker pale than the rest of his skin. "They already hate me, so why not let them hate me more? Brilliant logic, oh king of the gods."

"You can mock the logic, but it is sound." Odin looked him up and down. "I've not gotten the impression you even mind letting out the hostility I'm hearing right now, when the situation calls for it."

A rasp crept into Loki's voice. "I mind. I mind that I need to be angry at all. If I find ways to take a little joy in the dung-heap lot you've given me—"

"Loki." For the first time, Odin's full power thrummed through his words. Even now, even faced with just a memory, the trickster flinched. The ache in my gut dug deeper.

The Allfather straightened up even taller, looming beside his chair. "I asked this of you as one oath-brother to another. Do you think it doesn't pain me too? But what must be done... it must be done. I *need* you. I thought I could count on you. Was I wrong?"

Loki wet his lips. "No," he said, quieter now. "You weren't. I just don't understand. Why does any of this have to happen at all?"

"I've read the signs. Gleaned the omens. Unpuzzled the Norns tangled prophecies. This age is going to run itself down whether we like it or not. All we can do is end it well. A clean break. The realm cleansed in fire. I know you've got the spirit to lead that charge, don't you, trickster?" A dark gleam lit in the Allfather's one eye. "They need a villain. Who better could I have asked to play him?"

A chill ran down my back. Freya covered her mouth with a noise of shock. Thor's hand closed around mine so tight it almost hurt.

"And if I don't want to play that part?" Loki said.

"Then our fall may be that much more painful. Is

that what you'd rather instead?" Odin's gaze didn't waver.

"I never wanted any of it!" Loki shouted, shoving himself off the side of the chair. "There wasn't really any choice, was there? Be your villain or be a villain by betraying my oath to you. Either way, the world falls apart and it's all my fault. While you stand there with your damned knowing smile…"

Odin didn't even stir at his rant. I suspected the Loki back then hadn't been quite that scathing. Faced with that unwavering calm, the trickster's rage deflated. He looked suddenly beaten in a way I'd never seen before. The sight tore at my heart.

"You'll stay the course?" Odin said.

Loki swiped his hand across his face. "You see everything, don't you?" he said. "Past, present, and future, from the mouths of the Norns, from your fragments of prophecies… Somehow I think you already knew I would."

"Good." Odin set his hand on Loki's shoulder. "All Asgard will thank you in the end."

He picked up his hat and vanished back into the shadows. Loki raised his head to watch the Allfather go.

"Funny," he said. "That particular end is taking an awfully long time coming."

I couldn't stand to hang back any longer. I pulled my hand from Thor's and hurried across the room to Loki. He turned at the sound of my feet, hope and apprehension both flashing through his expression—as if he thought I might shy away from him again at the last second. My lungs contracted. I slipped my arms around him, tipping my head against his lean chest.

"I'm sorry," I said.

"Whatever for, pixie?" Loki said in his more usual light tone. "For believing me when I asked you to? For drawing the intended conclusions from the information you had? I don't see any crime in that." But his hand quivered a little as it stroked over my hair. I had the feeling the confrontation had taken more out of him than he was willing to show.

"Loki," Hod said, his voice rough, and then didn't seem to know how to go on.

"I didn't really let myself wonder why he stayed so close with you, after everything," Baldur said. "I never... I never would have thought he'd have wanted..."

"I don't think he did want any of it," Loki said. "He just saw it as the lesser of two evils. Fortunately for him, he had someone to deliver those evils and deflect the blame."

"When I can talk to my father for real..." Thor said gruffly, and Loki nodded.

Freya made a startled sound. "The walls," she murmured.

I looked up. As I did, the window across from me quavered. A waft of that ashy smell drifted in, along with red-tinted darkness. The real world beyond the construct.

All the gods could see it. They turned toward it as I stepped from Loki. But before I'd reached that breach, it shimmered away again.

Thor smacked his hammer against the wall. The

stones held. He frowned. "We're still just as trapped as ever."

Another spot on the wall twitched briefly open before my eyes. "No," I said. "We're not. She can shut us away in one place, but her prison is still breaking down. She's exhausted, and we keep changing our memories, and— If we could just wear them down a little more... We're almost out. I'd bet she can't do anything except hold this room in place as well as she can now, or she'd already have thrown us apart."

"What are you thinking, Ari?" Hod asked.

"I don't know. We get closer every time we shake up how we're thinking about the past. But I don't..."

I hesitated. There was another element to it. I'd seen it. Muninn hadn't opened up the floor in Hod's bedroom after we'd been together. The rush of emotion must have shaken her constructs too. Just like the illusion had fractured a sliver when I'd kissed Thor, when I'd started to get hot and heavy with Baldur. Because it focused us so completely on the sensations of the present? Because those feelings gnawed at Muninn's mind in some other way? I thought of the scene I'd witnessed, her curled up against the dying man.

There were people she'd cared for once. A man she'd loved.

But in the end it didn't really matter why. It only mattered that it worked. My heart started to beat faster.

We'd been through so much together. I shouldn't be afraid of this. I knew every man—every *god*—in this room. I knew they would never take anything except what I gave them freely. So why did the past hang over me like a goddamned anvil?

I dragged in a breath. We all had these stupid ideas about who we were, what we could and couldn't, do, weighing down on us, didn't we? I'd heard it from everyone around me in this room. Remembering that, an idea lit like a flame inside me. A flame that sent a flush of heat over my skin and a pulse of desire down through my belly.

"I need you," I said, looking to each of the gods in turn. "I need all of you."

The heat inside me carried through my words. Freya gave a soft cough. "I'll just be getting out of your way then."

Loki smirked as she slipped away into the darker side of the room, behind the chair. He stepped up beside me. Baldur and Thor joined him in a semi-circle around me, watching me with curious anticipation. Only Hod hung back, but just a little, his head cocked as if he were waiting to see where I was going with this.

Even though I'd already committed to this plan in my mind, I had to swallow before I spoke to make sure my voice didn't shake. "We aren't what anyone thought we were, are we? And we can show just how true that is."

"What did you have in mind, pixie?" Loki asked in a liquid murmur.

I balked, but only for a second. The second it took me to realize I knew exactly where to start. I grasped Baldur's hand and gave him a little tug to come even closer, holding his bright blue gaze so he'd see just how much I meant this.

"Baldur can be wicked."

Desire sparked in the light god's eyes. He bent to claim my mouth so swiftly I barely had time to breathe. His tongue teased my lips apart in an instant, his hand coming to my breast to pinch my nipple through my clothes. I gasped against his mouth as I arched into him. Urging, pleading with every movement for more.

He grazed his teeth down the side of my neck, offering shivers of pleasure with every nip, and I locked eyes with my trickster.

"Loki can be selfless," I murmured.

A grin stretched across his face. "Any time you like, my darling Ari."

As Baldur tugged up my shirt for better access to my breasts, Loki knelt before me. The light god rolled my other nipple, and Loki kissed the sensitive skin just below my belly button. He lingered there, flicking open the button of my jeans. A sudden flash of panic shot through me, but I shoved it down. I closed my eyes as he slid my jeans and panties down.

His lips charted a scorching path down my thigh and then up it again. By the time he reached the apex of my legs, I didn't have a shred of anything but wanting left in me. He brought his mouth right to my core, slicking his tongue over my clit, and I moaned.

It still wasn't enough. I looked to Thor through my haze of desire. His normally warm brown eyes were blazing as he gazed back at me. One of my hands was tangled in Baldur's shirt. The other I held out to the thunder god.

"Thor can be gentle."

He dropped his hammer on the floor and reached me in one quick stride. But when he rested his hand on my waist and brought his lips to mine, there was only tenderness in his touch. I lost myself in his kiss, in Baldur's strokes of my breasts, in Loki's hot mouth against my core. Bliss rippled through me from every direction.

When Thor raised his head to kiss my cheek, my temple, my gaze found Hod. And suddenly I wasn't sure what to say.

As if he'd sensed my dilemma, Hod smiled a little wryly. "Hod can bear witness," he said. "Without bitterness."

A sense of rightness settled in my chest. Then Baldur swept the peak of my breast into his mouth, testing it with his teeth, and Loki dipped a finger beneath the swipe of his tongue to hook up inside me, and Thor's large but careful hands caressed down my sides with the slightest shimmer of electricity. In that instant, I trembled with nothing but joy.

"And I am not a victim," I said, clutching Loki's silky hair, leaning into Thor's solid frame. "Not anymore. I take what I want."

And I wanted all of them. Oh, fucking yes. For the first time, the thought filled my mind without a hint of shame or fear. I gave myself over to it, to whatever would come next.

24

Thor

Ari moaned as she rocked in our joined embrace. I caught her mouth, keeping my kiss soft but sure. Her fiery sweet taste filled my senses. The feel of her naked skin against my bare chest misted my mind with a haze of lust, almost as potent as my battle rage. Lightning tickled through my veins, eager to spark from my fingers.

But I could hold my coarser urges in check. I *could* be the gentle lover she'd asked for from me. Baldur provoked a pleased cry from her with a squeeze of her breast, and I drew a whimper after it as I grazed my thumb over the other. When I trailed my mouth along the side of her jaw, she tipped her head to the side, offering better access to the pale line of her neck. Trusting me implicitly. My heart swelled at that gift.

Loki eased her thighs farther apart with a slick of his tongue I could hear. Ari gasped as he worked her over with hands and mouth. Her body started to tremble against mine. I held her, supporting her, drinking in the eager shivers with the press of my lips against the crook of her shoulder. She arched back with a clenching of the muscles all through her body. One hand clamped around my arm. I felt her release course through her.

The trickster kissed the side of her leg and straightened up with a sly smile. "And I ask nothing in return," he said.

He looked ready to step away, but Ari made a disgruntled sound and grasped the front of his shirt. She pulled him to her, into a kiss.

I'd come to women alongside Loki in the past, during our travels, but never for anything more than a quick roll in the hay. Ari was more than that—to all of us. But not even a flicker of jealousy rose in my chest. We'd all come together to bring her into our lives, and now she was a part of us just as we were a part of her. We were bound together in some strange way, both in battle and in desire. Watching Loki cup her face and kiss her back only made me wish I'd contributed just as much to her pleasure this time.

Maybe I could. When Ari let go of the trickster, she turned to me and tugged me into a kiss too. Her hand roamed over my chest, tracing heat everywhere it touched. My erection pulsed even harder in my pants. Damn, this woman was more intoxicating than any mead.

The valkyrie's hand slid all the way down to the waist of my pants. My breath hitched when she brushed her fingers over my groin. "I don't think we're done yet," she murmured, and kissed me again.

As my mouth melted against hers, she unfastened my belt. I couldn't hold back a groan. With a yank, she sent my jeans to my knees. Gentle. She wanted gentle. It should have been a challenge, but instead the thought sent a thrill of exhilaration through me. I could be the man she needed, even in this.

Baldur slid his arms around Ari's waist from behind. "Here," he said, with a smile that did look wicked, and hefted her onto the arm of Odin's high seat. The perfect height for her body to align with mine.

Ari grinned and wrapped her fingers around my straining cock. Hunger flooded my body. I kissed her tenderly but with all the longing I had in me, stroking her breasts, easing her hips a little closer to mine. Gently. Gently. Every soft movement, every second stretched out as I took my care with her, only made the heat of desire inside me flare brighter. Our tongues tangled, the faintest spark of electricity leaping between them, and she whimpered.

She was right. This was a part of me too: this passionate but steady man who had her quivering hungrily with just a brush of my fingertips. Right now, it was the only man I wanted to be.

Baldur knelt on the seat behind her. He nipped her shoulder as he gripped her ass, and Ari gasped into my mouth. Her body canted forward. She urged me to her, her hand still tight around my length, and rocked against the head of my cock.

Her frame was so small I had a moment's worry about whether I could give her what she was asking for without any pain, but her wetness slicked over me, her folds hot and ready, and skies above, there wasn't any bliss better than this.

I set one hand on her hips and let the other fall to the sensitive nub at her core. My thumb teased over it with another soft spark, earning me a moan from her. She arched toward me, and I sank into her, just the head. Her slick heat closed around me. I groaned into her hair.

"More," she said, gripping my shoulders. I let out a rough chuckle and shifted my hips. Inch by blissfully torturous inch, I slid deeper inside her. Then I eased back and plunged into her again. Ari gasped, clutching me tighter.

I found a rhythm, slowly building speed, penetrating her a little deeper with each thrust. Ari bucked to meet me. Her legs wrapped around my thighs and her mouth found mine again, our kisses ragged, broken by sounds of pleasure we couldn't contain.

I was bringing her that pleasure. I was sending her further into ecstasy with each measured roll of my hips. I sank into her all the way to the hilt, and she gave a cry that had nothing but joy in it.

"Next time I'll take the fierceness," she murmured against my shoulder. "I want every part of you."

The words sent a giddy tremor through me. I thrust faster, drinking in her scent, losing myself in the feel of her, and Ari came around me with a sharper cry. The clamp of her body around my cock stole the last of my control. My balls clenched, and I released my own ecstasy in a rush of crackling heat.

As the orgasm crashed through me like a wave, the walls around us toppled. The construct of the chair disintegrated into the air. I caught Ari against my body as we fell, slamming one arm out to deflect the impact. We pulled apart with a shared gasp.

"Well, well, well," Loki said, swiveling. "What have we here?"

The dark ragged walls of an immense cavern rose around us. Only a faint pulsing light gleamed over us from glowing patches of red in the ceiling high above. It all appeared to be a natural solid structure except for the wall to my right, where boulders jumbled against each other as if a landslide had covered the entrance.

Ari scrambled for her clothes. Her face was still flushed, but her eyes shone with determination rather than desire now. "We did it," she said. "We broke through."

I yanked up my pants and fastened my belt with a jerk. Mjolnir lay near my feet as if I'd set it down here and not in the room that had appeared as Odin's tower. I snatched it up with a preparatory swing.

"What is this place?"

"I smell ash," Hod said, his head cocked. "And sulfur."

"From that and the looks of the place, I'd say we've found ourselves in Muspelheim." Loki nodded to Ari. "The realm of fire. Not much lives here, at least not much we'd like to meet."

"This is the place I saw when I got into fragments of some of Muninn's memories," the valkyrie said. She extended her wings from her back with a burst of wind. The silver-white feathers glinted starkly in the ruddy light. Her jaw tightened. "Odin was here then, and he's still here now. I can feel him. That way." She pointed to the rockslide wall.

Freya brandished her sword. "Let's go before Muninn and whoever else she has on her side realize we've escaped."

The thought of my father brought back the conversation Loki had shown us in Odin's tower. The way the Allfather had spoken to the trickster... Could he really have *wanted* Loki to do all the things he had? To bring down all of Asgard? And not just wanted that, but forced Loki to keep up the role despite his protests.

The scene had felt true, and its veracity left a queasy sensation in my gut. But we weren't going to find any answers until we had the real Odin with us again. No matter what he'd done in the past, Muninn and the dark elves needed to fall right now for their many crimes.

I gripped the handle of my hammer hard. "I can clear the way."

I charged at the wall, the ground shuddering beneath my feet, and flung Mjolnir with all my strength. The hammer slammed into the mass of rock and blasted straight through it. Chunks of stone rained down on the cavern floor, and more of that reddish light flowed in through the hole, beckoning us.

Mjolnir flew back to my hand. I whipped it out again, smashing more of the rubble into pebbles. The higher boulders tumbled down and cracked open on the ground. With one last hurl, I shattered a clear path through the avalanche.

We rushed forward, Ari and Freya with their blades at the ready, Hod's shadows snaking around him. The six of us burst out onto a rocky plain overlooking a thick river of magma. A mountain rose on the other side of it, blocking off most of our view. Heat wafted up, drawing a layer of fresh sweat across my skin, for much less pleasurable reasons. My muscles tensed as I scanned the landscape.

"Can you still sense Odin?" Baldur asked Ari.

She turned slowly, her wings fluttering as if testing the air. Her forehead furrowed.

"Somewhere that way," she said, motioning toward the mountain with a frown. "I saw... He was in a cave, behind a waterfall of magma. If we can find that..."

Loki was already springing into the air. He strode up toward the sky with swift steps that covered a vast stretch in an instant. I was ashamed to find that even now, after everything he'd shown us, suspicion jabbed my gut—that he might be running off on his own, abandoning us.

If that scene had been true, then he'd never really been against us at all. He'd let us hate him to spare us pain. And I'd never even seen it. I'd have to be a better friend now.

High above us, the trickster's eyes narrowed with a flash. He glided back down at full speed.

"I see the place," he called. "Just beyond that ridge. Are we ready to fight?"

Freya brandished her sword. "Never more."

Hod was already collecting his shadows into a plane beneath his feet. Beside him, Baldur gleamed with his bright magic. Ari stretched her wings in anticipation.

"Whatever they've got waiting for us, it can't be

worse than what we've already beaten," she said. "We'll get to him this time."

All the battling I'd done in Muninn's prison had left me sore, but a surge of exhilaration ran through me. My fingers tightened around Mjolnir's handle. I had real enemies to fight here. Real enemies to *destroy* on our way to the Allfather. We would see him properly home this time.

For just a second, as the battle fury trickled through my thoughts, some part of me hesitated. A flicker of that more distant shame touched me. My gaze slid to Ari.

She smiled at me, her eyes as fierce and bright as the resolve inside me. Not a shred of fear or judgment in them.

"I think it's time to let that rage out," she said.

A different sort of pleasure rang through my nerves. Yes. I could be gentle, but I was a warrior too. And I'd never been more glad of that fact. Muninn and the rest would regret every bit of pain they'd dealt to me and mine.

With a battle cry, I leapt forward, letting the power of my fury carry me into the air after Loki.

25

Aria

The hot wind buffeted my wings as I propelled myself through the air. Who knew how much time we had, what other tricks Muninn and her allies might have planned? The sulfur stink filled my nose, but I kept my flaps strong and even. Rocky ground slipped by beneath me, but the dark craggy mountain ahead of us still seemed too far away.

"Is there anything I need to know about Muspelheim?" I called to the gods around me. For all my valkyrie powers, I was going to be the weakest link in this fight, and I was coming to it way too unprepared. I didn't want to make a mistake that screwed us over.

"There isn't much to the place beyond what you can see for yourself," Loki said, slowing his pace to fall in beside me. The wind rippled through his hair. He could have raced all the way to Odin's cage in a few minutes on his supernaturally enhanced shoes, I suspected, but trying to take on the rescue all by himself probably wasn't the wisest. "Harsh terrain, not much for sustenance. Home to rock dragons and stone spiders and not much else. Not anywhere we'd have thought to come looking."

"Why would the dark elves have brought Odin here?"

"So we wouldn't find him," Freya suggested. "You'd already tracked him to their realm. They knew we'd come there looking again."

"All the realms are connected by gates here and there," Hod said behind me. He'd be navigating from the sounds of the rest of our bodies in flight. "If they had a convenient gate, it wouldn't have taken much effort to send a force through it with him."

"I hate to think what they must have done to him that he couldn't escape, even when they had to move him to a new prison," Baldur said.

My memories of Odin, via Muninn's memories, trickled up through my mind. "I think they've had him a long time," I said. "You said he's been gone twice as long as ever before, right? That's, like, decades? When I saw him, from Muninn's eyes... he looked pretty beaten down."

"The Allfather can withstand more than any elf could deal out," Thor said gruffly, but his expression had darkened with worry.

Had Muninn known about the way the Allfather had used Loki, the destruction he'd encouraged behind the other gods' backs? She must have, with all the time she'd used to spend at Odin's side. One more reason for her to resent him. I wasn't sure how much I was looking forward to meeting the guy properly, after everything I'd seen.

But we needed Odin to get us out of here and to the real Asgard. That was all that mattered for now.

"This way," Loki called, swerving to the right. We veered after him, seconds before a spurt of fire speared up from the ground, close enough that my skin prickled with its heat.

I squeezed my fingers around the handle of my switchblade. It wasn't much of a weapon compared to swords or enchanted hammers or blasts of magic, but it was mine. It held all the love Francis had put into that gift. Even if I wasn't sure I could take on a rock dragon, whatever the hell that was, with it, it did sometimes come in handy for directing my sporadic bolts of lightning as well.

Another river of magma flowed around the side of the mountain through the same passage I guessed we'd fly through. The prickling of heat sank down to my bones. Was that the same spot where I'd seen Odin ambushed?

It had definitely been somewhere here, in the red glow of Muspelheim, not in Nidavellir's more cramped and shadowy caves. Muninn had led him *here* for his enemies to fall on him. So, transporting him here hadn't just been a last-ditch attempt to hide him. They had some kind of tie to this place too.

"We should fly high above that chasm," I hollered into the wind, pointing. "I don't think we want to find ourselves closed in."

Loki nodded without hesitation. As we all pulled higher from the ground, Baldur drew up beside me. He looked as if he were soaring along on a beam of light. Which possibly he was. He reached his hand out to me, and I caught it, twining my fingers with his for the few moments before I had to let go to keep my flight steady.

"I realized I should say thank you," he said, only loud enough for me, not the others, to hear. "Before we face whatever's waiting for us over there."

I glanced over at him, startled. "Thank me for what?"

He beamed back at me—the bright soft smile I was used to, not the slightly wicked one I'd learned I could tempt out with the right inspiration. It didn't look as dreamy as it used to, I noticed with a little relief. Muninn might have tortured him with his memories of his death, but he seemed to have come out of it stronger. Better able to face the reality in front of him without shying away from the shadows.

"You helped me find pieces of myself I didn't know were there," he said. "Maybe I've got a bit of darkness in me too. That's useful to know."

"More useful to me than you so far," I couldn't help responding. The memory of our encounter in Odin's tower flooded me with heat. I'd given myself over to pleasure like I'd never dared to before... and now I felt even more like myself. There were pieces of me that deserved more time in the open too, pieces *I'd* shied away from too long.

A hint of that wickedness crept into Baldur's expression. "I am hoping we'll have plenty of time to explore that side more," he said with a wider grin.

So was I. Oh, so was I.

"Ari, what else did you see in the scraps of memory you got from Muninn?" Thor called over. "What's waiting for us?"

"I don't know exactly," I said. "There were different bits that I think must have been from different times." I couldn't even say they were all from the week or two since the dark elves and whoever else must have moved Odin here from the elvish caves, if he'd been held here when they'd first captured him too. "He was trapped in a heavy-looking cage in that cave behind the magma flow. When I saw him there, he was alone or it was just Muninn there with him. It's possible they think he's hidden away well enough that they're not bothering to guard him."

At that moment, Loki pulled a little higher from where he was gliding along in the lead. His inhumanly sharp eyes narrowed. "Not anymore," he said. "There's your magma flow—and there's an army waiting for us around it."

I pushed myself faster to catch up with him, to see what he did. Beyond the tighter passage beside the mountain, the landscape opened up into a sprawl of plains and blood-red streams. A cliff stood farther back to our right, magma spilling in a churning torrent down its face. It flowed on into the river we'd been following at the cliff's base.

At first, the ground around that river looked as if a thick shadow was spread across it. Then the shadow twitched. I focused my own enhanced vision as intently as I could and caught the stirring of human-like forms.

"We can fly right over them," Thor said.

"But not over that dragon." Freya pointed with her sword.

A huge beast was unfurling its body by the edge of the cliff. Until it had moved, I'd have thought it was just part of the rock. Its stone-like scales shifted over its sinewy body, a reddish gleam showing along the seams. Another flew into view, heading toward us with wing-strokes so powerful they made the air warble. Two more joined it as the one on the cliff lifted into the air as well. The closest one opened its maw with a blech of flame I could feel even at a distance.

A shudder ran down my back. I couldn't fight those things, no.

Thor was already charging to meet them. He swung his brawny arm, sending his hammer flying. It struck the closest dragon across the skull. The creature flinched but pushed forward, faster, with a roar—right into a clot of shadow Hod had summoned. The streaks of darkness twisted around it, pinning its wings to its body, clamping around its jaws. It plummeted from the sky into the molten river below.

The other three dove at us. Freya sliced her sword through the air with a muttered magical line. Baldur hurled a streak of light in unison. Her conjured force and his brilliant magic struck the second dragon at the same time, cracking its belly open. Thor finished the job with a slam of his hammer right between its eyes.

Loki gave a shout, darting beneath a swipe of another dragon's claws. "Fire doesn't hurt these menaces," he said. "If someone could lend a hand..."

Hod threw a ball of shadow his way. Thor wheeled with his hammer. And the fourth dragon streaked up from below, straight for Freya.

She whipped around, but I could tell it wouldn't be fast enough. Not letting myself think, I threw myself forward, lashing out with my switchblade.

It glanced off the monster's side, and the dragon's barbed paw smacked into me, sending me spinning in the air. Pain jabbed down my side, but I'd distracted it enough for Freya to dodge. Thor rammed his hammer into the dragon's chest, and Baldur hurled another bolt of light at the other.

The two beasts whipped between us, one's tail slashing across Loki's chest, the other's jaws scraping across Hod's shoulder as he wrenched himself out of the way. *No.* I whirled around, and the gods lunged into fighting stances.

For an instant, all of us moving at the same time toward the same goal, a weird sense of power hummed through me, as if I could taste Hod's shadows, Baldur's light, Loki's fire, and Thor's brutal strength, lancing through my body and back to them.

I swept my arm in the hopes that the fickle lightning might streak from my hand. It didn't, but as the gods attacked too, magic exploded in the air all around us. Light streaked with fire whipped across one dragon's face. Mjolnir careened into the other dragon's belly with a stream of shadow that wrenched through the creature's scales. A bolt of flaming darkness seared down its maw, choking it as it started to fall. A ball of light slammed into the first dragon's jaw with the force of a hammer, splitting its head down the middle.

We all paused, a little stunned, as the dragons plummeted to their deaths. "What in Hel's name just happened there?" Thor demanded.

Loki regained his composure with a breathless chuckle. "I have no idea, but I'm thinking the time for sorting it out is *after* we've fought the rest of the battle, not before."

The army around the cliff looked as if it were swarming right into the rock. I shook off the hum still tingling through my limbs with renewed urgency. "There must be caves there leading up to the one Odin is trapped in," I said. "They're going to grab him." And do who knew what to him. Kill him, if they could, before we got to him? Drag him off someplace else so we'd have to go through this all over again trying to track him down?

Thor hurled himself forward with a roar that could have rivaled the dragons'. It reverberated through the air as we charged after him. We swooped down over the landscape toward the gap between the falling magma and the crevice I could now make out behind it. The twang of my connection to Odin rippled through me. He was still there—for now.

Spindly black shapes wriggled across the cliff-face. Creatures like enormous spiders, I saw as we flew near. They sprang off the rock at us as we raced toward the cave.

A yelp escaped me as one caught me, its wiry jointed legs clamping around my wings like a vise. I slammed my elbow into it, my knife into the huge faceted eye that stared blankly at me. Black liquid hissed up out of the wound, but its legs didn't budge. I was dropping out of the sky, falling way too fast toward that cracked stone ground—

A streak of flame blasted the creature right off me. Loki caught my hand, yanking me upright as I found my wings. "No ducking out of this one, pixie," he said in his teasing lilt. "Come on."

We hurtled after the others through the opening, into the cave. The battle was already raging. Mjolnir glinted in the hazy red light, and beams of Baldur's summoned light glanced off the jagged walls. I caught a gleam off the tarnished bars of a cage—Odin's cage—back in the depths of the cave. A horde of dark elves and other figures in sooty armor clogged the space between us and the Allfather.

But it was him—the real him. His presence echoed through me, yanking me onward with even more might.

I hit the ground with both feet and slashed out with my knife. The shadows inside me, the ones that could claim lives with the power Hod had given me, stirred eagerly surrounded by so many living, breathing foes with actual glimmers of life, not the hollow constructs I'd had to tackle in Muninn's prison.

I wrenched my hand across one warrior's head and slammed it into another's chest, snatching away the energy that sustained them like the valkyrie I was. In another age, it'd have been my duty to decide who lived and who fell, and which of the fallen ascended to the great hall of Valhalla.

All of these jerks could just forget about that.

As I rammed and wrenched my way through the crowd, that weird hum resonated through me again. The ripples of magic around me wavered and collided. Light and shadow and fire ricocheted off each other with twice their original force, blasting through the horde.

I caught sight of Thor's puzzled face in the fray, twisting with fury a second later. Mjolnir slammed through the crowd, sizzling with fiery light as it toppled every figure in its path.

A hoarse shout rang out somewhere in the depths of the cave. "Retreat! The word is to retreat! Leave him! We'll make good on this another day."

The horde surged away from us. A flutter of movement caught my eye. A black form swooped by along the ceiling of the cave. For the briefest moment, the raven's eye met mine. Then Muninn was bolting away with the rest of the army.

I soared after them, but the moment I reached the cage, my wings faltered. Something in my chest shivered and then stilled at the sight of Odin's hunched form.

His hand shot out to grip one of the bars. His head raised, just enough for the glint of his single eye to show beneath the wilted brim of his hand.

"Valkyrie," he rasped, with a voice that seemed to burrow right through me.

"It's him," I gasped out, unable to tear my gaze from him. "It's really Odin." I knew that down to the smallest bone in my body.

"Father," Thor said in a voice rough with horror. He bashed Mjolnir into the bars of the cage. They shook and cracked. With another heave, he'd battered the cage right open.

"Well," Loki said, weary but relieved, as Freya ducked in to throw her arms around her husband, "I have to say I've had quite enough of all this. What do you say we really go home this time?"

26

Aria

I woke up feeling as if I'd been asleep for days. For the first few minutes, I couldn't quite bring myself to even roll over. The plump mattress I was lying on, the soft blanket I was lying under, were just too damned comfortable. My muscles ached, but it was the dull ache of hard work now over with, not the sharp ache of fresh pains. I kind of liked the sensation.

My memories of the last short journey from Muspelheim were hazy. We'd helped Odin out of that cage, flown him up to the top of the cliff, and from there he'd managed to summon forth a shaky bridge up through the clouds that clotted the dark sky. As I'd realized we really were done, all the fighting was over, my eyelids had already been drooping. I had a vague recollection of an arm coming around my back to support some of my weight, eerily familiar stone halls coming into view around a marble-tiled courtyard... and after that I drew a blank.

So, where the hell was I? My heart lurched. I pushed back the blanket and sat up.

The bed was in a plain room, small but with a high ceiling. The stone-block walls told me it was probably one of the Asgardian halls. One of the real ones, that wouldn't upend me without warning. What looked like morning sunlight spilled across the smooth stone floor from a narrow window. A padded chair stood in one corner, and a low teak dresser sat against the opposite wall. No sound carried from outside the room.

I breathed in deep, and my heightened valkyrie senses caught a faint whiff of a tangy smoky smell. Oh. I was pretty sure I knew whose guest room I'd ended up in.

Cautiously, I slipped out of the bed and padded into the hall. A glance down it resonated with my memories. Yep, this was Hod's home.

I eased past a couple of doors to one that was only slightly ajar. Nudging it open, I found what had to be the master bedroom, twice as big as the one I'd left with a bed twice as large. Hod was sprawled on it, the blanket tangled around his waist, his lean chest and shoulders bare. In sleep, his face had softened. It was easier to see the resemblance to his twin now.

I hesitated, but the pang inside me pushed me onward. After everything I'd just been through, I didn't want to sit alone in one of his barely familiar rooms waiting for him to wake up.

After everything we'd been through together, I didn't think he'd mind the intrusion.

The door squeaked faintly as I ducked inside, but the dark god didn't stir. I clambered onto the bed and curled up next to him, inhaling his salty smoky smell up close now.

The mattress shifted with my movement, and Hod woke up with a backwards jerk, his body tensing.

Shit. "Hey, it's just me," I said, my face flaring. This wasn't the gentle morning welcome I'd been picturing.

Hod's shoulders had already come down. "My spare bed wasn't good enough for you, valkyrie?" he muttered, but he scooted closer at the same time, looping his arm around my waist to tug me to him, back to front. I smiled, nestling into his warmth. This was more like it.

"Sorry," I said. "I didn't mean to startle you."

"Not used to having anyone else in my bed," Hod said. He tucked his chin over my shoulder, his breath tickling over my hair.

"Is that something you'd like to change?" I murmured suggestively, and felt him smile.

He kissed the corner of my jaw, that tiny gesture sending a flare of heat through me. "I could get used to this, I think."

"We could try it a few times, just to be sure."

"Would *you* want to?"

I paused, reveling in how comfortable lying here with him was, how protected I felt tucked in against him. "Yeah. I think I would."

"I suppose your other suitors might take issue with you playing favorites," Hod said.

I rolled my eyes. "I didn't make any promises about this being the *only* bed I'd ever share."

"Huh. Next thing I know, you'll be wanting to invite them all over."

"That's a brilliant idea!" I said brightly. "There's room for more. Let me go get them right now."

"Don't you dare."

"You going to stop me?"

I made as if to squirm off the bed, biting back a giggle. Hod gave a low growl and grabbed me. He rolled on top of me, his head dipping down as if to claim a kiss, which was exactly what I'd been angling for, but the second I felt his weight pressing down on me, my body went rigid.

He pulled back in an instant. "Ari?"

My pulse had hiccupped, but it was already falling back into its usual steady rhythm. I dragged in a breath. "I'm okay. Just... got a little overconfident. I guess it'd be a little much to hope every bad reaction disappeared in an instant." I gave a little laugh. "Looks like we both still have crap to get over."

"Hmm." He sank back down beside me and stroked the back of his fingers down the side of my face. My throat tightened. I nudged myself closer to him again, turning toward him this time, and leaned my head against his chest.

"We've come a long way," he said after a moment. "Haven't we?"

"Yeah, I'd say we have."

"Then we'll just keep healing. Together." He brushed his thumb over my cheek. "No tears this time. That's a definite step in the right direction."

"Keep talking like that and they'll come," I grumbled.

He chuckled and tipped my chin up. This time when

he moved to kiss me, no impulse ran through me except the urge to kiss him back.

The heat of his mouth radiated all the way through my body. I let myself linger there, trading breaths and the caress of our lips, until a sharper heat started to pool low in my belly. I slid my hand down Hod's chest—and the sense of a summons reverberated through my head as if someone had shouted my name.

I sat up, touching my forehead. The sensation came again, like an insistent tug. It echoed down through my chest to the place where I'd felt Odin's presence before.

"I think Odin is calling for me," I said. I wasn't sure I liked this new feature of being a valkyrie—the Allfather having a direct line to my brain.

Hod pushed himself upright beside me with a sigh. "I'd better come too, then. He wasn't in much of a state last night to discuss what he'd been through. Maybe now he can tell us more about who captured him and why."

I enjoyed the view as he pulled on more clothes, grimacing when the call came again. "All right, all right," I said to Odin, who probably couldn't hear my answer anyway.

Hod led the way out into Asgard, his strides smooth and unguarded now that he could trust his home to stay as it was meant to. As we approached the huge hall at the far end of the city, the one with a higher tower rising from its rooftop, uneasiness coiled through my gut. I might not have really met the Allfather properly yet, but I'd seen an awful lot of Odin in the last day. And an awful lot of what I'd seen hadn't sat quite right.

"It has to be true, right?" I said. "What Loki showed

us. Odin *told* Loki to make trouble, to push back against the gods..."

Hod was silent for a moment. "My father has always kept his own counsel," he said. "Or at least he did from his sons. But I know there was a lot he knew that gnawed at him—I've wondered how long he anticipated Ragnarok's coming. Whatever he did, whatever he asked Loki to do, it's because he thought it was best for all of us. I'm sure of that. Whether I agree with him that it was best..."

He couldn't seem to finish that sentence. No wonder. I couldn't imagine how much he was grappling with right now. It was his *father* he'd just had all these revelations about.

I found myself holding my breath as we pushed open the hall's front door. "In here," called the low dry voice that was somehow totally familiar even though I'd only heard it once in reality before this moment. After all, it was the same low dry voice that had commanded Loki to be his villain.

Odin sat in a tall, intricately carved chair in a room that felt like a miniature version of Valhalla. Spears and swords decorated the walls. The almost-throne was the only seat other than a few cushions in the corners. Baldur and Freya were poised at the Allfather's sides, Freya clasping her husband's hand and Baldur resting his fingers on his father's forearm.

They must have spent much of the night tending to the king of the gods, because years of fatigue and hurt had shed from Odin's posture, from his face. He sat straight, his broad shoulders squared, and his single eye twinkled with more energy than I'd have thought he could ever be capable of again after seeing him in that cage. The authority of his presence filled the room. A tremor that was more apprehension than anticipation tickled down my back.

Loki and Thor stood a short distance away. The thunder god shot me a smile, and the trickster gave me a nod and a wink. We were all assembled now before the Allfather.

"My son and my unexpected valkyrie," Odin said in greeting. He leaned back in his chair. "I wanted you all here while we speak of the battle to come."

My heart sank, my worries about the god in front of me momentarily pushed aside. "Didn't we win that battle?" I said.

But even as the words came out, I was remembering the human bodies slumped in the dark elves' caves, the missing persons signs, the voice calling for yesterday's army to retreat, promising to fight to the end another day. The dark elves had been doing a lot more than keeping Odin captive. They'd kidnapped humans and killed them and who knew what else or why.

Of course it wasn't over. There was so much evil we hadn't even tackled yet.

Odin's mouth twitched slightly upward. "We won something," he said. "I am ever grateful for my freedom. I wish I could say it came with peace. But Surt has bigger plans than that."

The name meant nothing to me, but the gods around me stiffened, even Loki. "What does that bastard have to do with this?" he said.

"He's the one who ordered my capture," Odin said. "With the help of my former raven of memory, it seems." He rubbed his mouth.

"Um... Who is Surt?" I ventured.

"A giant who led an army into Asgard and set the city up in flames," Freya said, her voice strained. "He killed my brother. He destroyed everything."

"But the city and we returned," Odin said, squeezing her hand. "And so did Surt. I shut him away in Muspelheim for his role in that uprising ages ago. It seems he's been stewing in his resentment of me and the rest of Asgard ever since."

"We stopped him," Thor said. "We retrieved you. What is there left that he can do?"

"Oh, there's plenty." The Allfather exhaled like a sigh. "Surt has been building his new army for a long time. He's allied with the dark elves and gathered the stragglers who've found their way into Muspelheim. But he knew that wasn't enough for his ultimate goal. So he's started summoning draugar to do his bidding too."

Hod set his hand on my shoulder, gripping tight. "The dead risen back to life," he said in a haunted tone.

Like that construct of Baldur rising up, lurching and rotten. A zombie. *Draug*, they'd called it. My stomach twisted.

The bodies I'd seen in the caves—the people they'd stolen—it all made a sudden sick kind of sense. They were building an army of the dead. Of *human* dead.

"And what does he mean to do with this horde of the undead?" Loki waved toward the doorway. "There's not that much in Asgard to claim these days."

"He'd be happy just to see our home torn from us," Odin said. "But that's not his only goal. It seems the balance of the nine realms has shifted. Many of them have become unstable. All except for Asgard, because of our power... and Midgard, at the center of it all. He plans to conquer the realm of humankind for his own purposes too."

A spear of ice jabbed through me at those words. This powerful giant wanted to conquer Midgard. And, what, set my former home up in flames? Turn it into a wasteland like the realm he ruled over now?

Petey was down there, with no one who knew anything to protect him...

My hands clenched. Each of the gods around me had glanced at me as if thinking the same thing.

I couldn't expect them to care about those lands half as much as I did, but I knew, with a faint whisper of hope under the balling of my gut, that they'd fight just as hard regardless. They'd stand by me, the four lovers who were connected to me in that strange balance of our own.

I stepped forward. "We have to stop him."

Odin bowed his head. "Yes," he said. "I agree. Which is why you're all here. We need to make our mark in this war *now*."

He really smiled then: a slow dark smile that curved his lips at a crooked angle. It sent a chill over my skin.

We'd come together. We'd saved Odin. But who was really more dangerous: the giant scheming in the realm of fire or the god we'd just rescued from him?

ABOUT THE AUTHOR

Eva Chase lives in Canada with her family. She loves stories both swoony and supernatural, and strong women and the men who appreciate them. Along with the Their Dark Valkyrie series, she is the author of the Witch's Consorts series, the Dragon Shifter's Mates series, the Demons of Fame Romance series, the Legends Reborn trilogy, and the Alpha Project Psychic Romance series.

Connect with Eva online:
www.evachase.com
eva@evachase.com

Printed in Great Britain
by Amazon